Good Girlz With Hood Habits 2

Welcome Home Kei'

By

Erica Dyer

ISBN 978-1-7361999-5-4

Library of Congress Catalog Card Number 2021907500

Good Girlz With Hood Habits 2: Welcome Home Kei'

Written by: Erica Dyer

Cover Design: GermanCreative

Website: www.ericareads.com

Last time......

Bishop

"Marry me, Kei," I said as we laid in the aftermath.

"You serious, Bishop?"

"Yeah, you it for me. Let's do it today."

"Bishop, I'll marry you right now, but I want you to be sure this is your heart talking and not your dick."

"Girl, I knew I wanted to marry you the day I first met you."

She laughed, "Bishop, I'll marry you under one condition." With that, I looked at her with a raised eyebrow.

"We wait a year before we tell anyone, and then we have a big ceremony."

"Why can't we tell nobody?"

"I want us to enjoy each other without other people's opinions."

"You haven't been wrong so far, baby girl, so I'm following your lead. But we are getting married today. Now get over here and suck me up like I like it." She didn't hesitate to put my dick in her mouth. Damn, I love this girl.

Kei'sha

Now all y'all judgmental people can kiss my ass. Yes, I did some risky shit for my nigga, but hell, I put us in a better position to win in life and upgraded my nigga. How many of you hoes can say that? Bishop was that nigga before, I just elevated him a little, and in return, he gave me his last name. That's right; I'm married now. Tiff and Sin were our witnesses; no one else knew, and I was serious about that one-year condition with Bishop. The wedding was short and sweet.

As we were walking out of the courthouse, gunshots started going off. Bishop used his body to cover mine. The shooting got closer and closer to us. "Kei, stay low and get back in the building." "Fuck no, I'm not leaving you out here; come in with me." Bishop must have lost his mind if he thought I was leaving him out here naked. He didn't have a gun on him, and neither did Sin. As soon as he was about to say something, a bullet hit him in his back.

"OMG Bishop, Bishop, get up, baby. Please get up." As I was screaming and crying, I noticed a figure getting close to me. I looked up, and it was crazy ass, Eric.

"You, stupid bitch I could have given you the world, and you went and married this trash."

"Eric, what are you doing here? You shot my husband!" I screamed.

"Oh, shut up, he's not dead, but he will be if you don't get your ass in this car now."

"I'm not going anywhere with you, you crazy bastard."

He shot Bishop in his leg.

"Next time, I'm going to shoot him in his head. Now let's go Bitch!"

I looked at Bishop briefly and got up with tears in my eyes as Eric pulled my hair and forced me into his car.

"I'm going to show you I am the man you need, but first, I need you relaxed for this flight."

"Flight, where are you taking me, Eric?"

"Away from here."

He stabbed me with a syringe, and within a matter of seconds, I was out cold.

Bishop

"Sir, I need you to get back in the bed; you cannot leave this hospital. Do you realize you've been shot several times?"

"With all due respect, lady, I know that, but I gotta find my wife!" I didn't mean to scream at the little white bitch, but I needed her to understand I was nothing without my wife. Kei' told me about that crazy nigga Eric but I never even thought this shit would happen. Right when I was about to zap again, Sin and Tiff walked in. "Y'all find her?"

"Yeah, bro, we found her, but you are not going to like where she's at."

"Sin, don't play with me. Where the fuck is my wife?"

"Bro, he took her to Cuba."

"Cuba, what the fuck!" I screamed before I passed out. My damn wife was gone.

To be continued

Welcome Home Kei'

2019

Kei'sha

"Bri'annna, put your sister down before you drop her," I told my 5-year-old as I walked into the backyard. "Bishop, I know you see her, right?"

"Kei, she's fine. I wasn't going let her drop her chill out."

Bri'annna and Kei'anna were 5 and 3, and you would have thought Bri'annna was her mother. She was overprotective and wouldn't let anyone besides the family touch her. It was so bad we had to take them out of the same school because Bri'annna would leave her Pre-K class to sit with Kei'anna in her head start class and wouldn't move until the day was over.

Tomorrow is Bri'annna's 6th birthday, and we are setting our backyard up for the party. Bishop brought me a 5-bedroom, 3.5-bathroom townhouse downtown near the Inner Harbor about a year ago. I would have been perfectly fine with our condo, but he and the other guys in our family thought it would be best if we all lived near each other. Our home is perfect. There's a man cave for Bishop, a playroom for the girls, along with office space for me. The girls each had their own room; however, Bri' always slept in KJ's room (we called Kei'anna KJ cause she is a splitting image of me). Bishop had the wall knocked down that separated the girl's room, so now they have one big ass room. Our life has changed so much in the last six years. After Cuba, Bishop and I went on an emotional rollercoaster, landing me in therapy.

I switched careers and became a stay-at-home mother and wife. Bishop wouldn't have it any other way. We opened a gym that held a private gun range and named it after the son we lost. "BJ's" was my pride and joy. We had an open gym on the first floor, all the exercise equipment you could think of on the second floor, and on the third floor, there was a boxing club. In the building's basement, the gun range was soundproof, bulletproof, and not on any blueprints of this building. Our gun range was the best-kept secret in Baltimore.

A lot of shit went down in Cuba that changed me. Even more shit went down when we came home. Bishop and I almost lost each other. Coming out of a situation like that can be traumatic

for anyone; however, we dealt with it. Bishop was right by my

side the whole time, even when I pushed him away. I guess I

better tell y'all all the shit that went down. Well, hold on; it's

going to be a bumpy ride.

Six years ago

Gisella Blanca

"What's wrong? Why are you here? Is the family okay?"

"I came here to get your help with Trevor, but we have bigger problems. Kei'sha has been kidnapped."

"Eboni, what do you mean Kei'sha has been kidnapped?"

"From what I gather, her ex-boyfriend from college shot her new husband as they were leaving the courthouse and kidnapped her. Kei'sha's husband is in a coma, and Kei'sha has been taken to Cuba."

"Cuba! Eboni, you are the oldest. How did this happen? And what do you mean you came here for Trevor? Where is Naheem?"

"Naheem is still in jail. Trevor was arrested and given six months in BCDC. We were fine at first, but Trevor has a loyalty to the Knight family that put him in a fucked-up position."

"Did you say, Knight? As in Mablevi Knight?"

"Yeah, that's him. You know him?"

"Yeah, I need you to get Laylani here now! Along with London and Lauren's asses, I'll call Paul myself. It's about time this family stop with all the fucking secrets."

"Gigi, Lay is dealing with some shit too, and she's pregnant."

"I know what Lay ass has going on; just get her here now!

"Gigi, how am I supposed to get her from California to Florida in a matter of minutes?"

"Eboni, you got 24hrs to get them all here. I have to make some calls."

"Mablevi! What the hell is going on? Why is Eboni here talking about Kei'sha is kidnapped, Trevor is locked up, and Bishop is in a comma?"

"Gisella, calm down. I have everything under control."

"No, Mablevi, I've let you be in control for far too long. You were supposed to make sure all of the kids were out of this life we built while I took the heat and went on the run. Do they even know that they're all god-brothers and sisters? And does Bishop know?"

"Gisella, these kids are grown and decided to get into this life. I didn't force it on them. The thing with Trevor is minor and will be handled in the next week. They all have bonds with each other. They know you as their godmother, but not that I'm their godfather. As for Bishop, no one knows he's your nephew."

"Mablevi, everyone needs to be here in the next 24hrs, or I'm coming out of hiding, and we both know if I come out of hiding, there's going be some slow singing and flower bringing. Now get here!"

I guess I better introduce myself. My name is Gisella Maria Aricka Blanca. You heard about me but now let me tell you my story. I won't take much of your time. I'm just here to explain my connection with everyone. As you know, I'm Eboni's godmother, along with Naheem's. What you don't know is Laylani, Kei'sha, Moshi, Paul, London, Lauren, and Purnell are also my godchildren. Clearly, I'm not your average godparent. I'm more of the behind-the-scenes type. I pay for tuition, buy gifts, and kill a motherfucker when needed. Eboni and Naheem are my oldest two god kids. Therefore, a lot of pressure has been placed on them to make sure nothing happens in my absence. Well, from what I hear, they have failed that mission— anyway, getting back to my story. I was born and raised in Spanish Harlem with my uncle and aunt, under the impression that our family was the average family. My uncle owned a bodega on 1st street, and my aunt worked at a factory. Nothing to fancy, we didn't have designer clothes, but we always dressed nicely and never went without.

When I turned 12, a man I barely remembered came and picked my brother, my sister, and myself up and moved us to Baltimore. That man was Alejandro Blanca, our father. He spent ten years in jail for man slaughter. The story is that my mom left my father to be with another man right after I was born. In the beginning, he was great; according to my older brother, the guy would take us all out, buy us stuff, and told my mom she didn't have to work anymore. However, after about a year, he became abusive, controlling, and started drinking a lot. One day the abuse went too far, and he choked our mother to death. My older brother AJ called our dad, and when he got there, he saw my mom lying dead in our living room and snapped. He killed the guy and was sent to jail. Luckily, my older brother, who was eight at the time, told the police what happened and that helped our father from getting life in prison for 1st-degree murder.

Our uncle Gabriel took us in and raised us until our dad was released. My brother started working with my dad and made a name for himself as a Lt in our dad's criminal empire. My older sister Gabriella took our new life and status and ran with it. She was 16 when we moved to Baltimore. Switching up her basic wardrobe to skimpy clothes and high heels, Gabriella gained attraction from older men. One man, in particular, was Brian King. He was a low-level drug dealer but was always in the mix. Brian was a few years older than Gabriella and had her wrapped around his finger. Our father did not approve of the relationship. He felt Brian wasn't good enough for his daughter, and to be honest, he was right. Brian was more into scamming

and stealing. He would take my sister on some of his missions,

putting her in harm's way. In the mix of robbing and stealing,

the water-downed Bonnie and Clyde duo got pregnant.

Gabriella gave birth to a little boy, Bishop Alejandro King. The

first two years of Bishop's life, Gabriella and Brian lived in our

home.

I loved my nephew. He was so smart and handsome. Right

around Bishop's 3rd birthday, Brian stole a kilo of coke and $50k

from my father's safe. Had it not been for Gabriella and Bishop,

my father would have killed Brian, but he didn't. Instead, he

told Gabriella that she was no longer welcomed in our home as

long as she stayed with Brian. Gabriella and Bishop left, but we

stayed in contact with each other. I talked to my sister every

day for the first three months after leaving, but then the calls

stopped. No one would answer the door when I went to visit

their apartment. One day I got a collect call from Gabriella; she

had been arrested. Come to find out, Brian and Gabriella were getting high and were doing bad. My brother AJ bailed her out, and Bishop came to live with us while Gabriella checked into rehab. That didn't last long.

One day while I was in school, Gabriella left rehab and came and got Bishop. We didn't hear anything from her for a while until one night; my dad got a call saying Gabriella was killed. Brian had taken Gabriella with him to rob a dealer in Park Heights, both of them were high as a kite, and the dealer ended up killing Gabriella. After her funeral, Bishop was back with us, but my brother and dad got knocked and were given football numbers. I was only 17 at the time. I tried to keep Bishop and the family business running, but I was better at selling dope than changing diapers. So, I made a deal with Brian that if he got cleaned and took care of my nephew, I would support him financially.

Everything was going well until Brian started committing check fraud. I had to bail him out so many times it was ridiculous.

Along with Brian's bull shit, I dealt with rival dealers coming at me, trying to kill me. One day when I had Bishop, this dealer named Shabazz shot at me in the middle of the damn playground. After that, I decided I would stay away from Bishop until I could guarantee his safety. I was a very ruthless woman. I had to be. Because of that, I always had a target on my back. Walking away from Bishop was the hardest thing I ever did in my life. He was like my own son. But I knew it was best for him. I still sent money and would show up now and then. After a while, I stopped going around altogether, and he forgot about me. The last time I interacted with my nephew was on his 5th birthday. His father was a pain in my ass for years. He was taking my money and spending it on women, liquor, and weed. By the time Bishop was 12, I was in charge of the entire Blanca family's criminal empire. I branched out in different countries, made allies with other criminal families, and had a solid crew holding me down.

Kendrick Williams and Mablevi Knight became my partners and friends. Mablevi was a coke dealing African living in Miami, and Kendrick was moving weight in Miami and New York with his brother's help. We all met through a mutual business associate. Mablevi and I tried to have a romantic relationship at first. I must admit it was good; however, we learned that we worked better at getting money together than being together. Mablevi became my connect, and Kendrick became my right-hand man. We were making money and living well. I was killing the game in Baltimore, Kendrick and Mablevi had the nightlife and drug game in Miami in a frenzy, and our little operation in NYC was doing pretty good as well. That is until Kendrick got knocked for tax invasion, money laundering, and terrorist financing. He had his family move to New York with his brother, where his wife Kemetria took over his part, and we became best friends.

Mablevi married and had three kids, Kendrick and Kemetria had four kids, I didn't have any kids and never planned on having any. Instead, I took on the role of godmother to other children.

When Kendrick got knocked, I moved to Miami. The business down there brought in more money and was bigger than our DMV region. My godson Naheem and Paul stayed with me (Paul's Kendrick's oldest son). We had a well-oiled machine for about three years until I was caught up in a setup with a trusted worker and the police. I shot my way out of the ordeal but was on the run for years. I hopped from Florida to the DMV, to Mexico, to New York, back to Florida. That's where I have been for the last 10-15 years, living in the hidden Indian Mounds of the Upper Sugarloaf Keys. There is no public entry to my home. It's not on any map, and it is underground, and with Eboni coming here pregnant is a serious risk for her and the baby. Having everyone coming to me is putting my freedom at risk as well, but too much shit has been going down with this family, and it's time to get the shit together.

"Laylani Williams, let me get this straight you were getting your ass beat for years and never told anyone? Then when you get out of that situation, you fall for a dude locked up that had you bringing in drugs risking your freedom, got you pregnant, still married, and fucking a girl you thought was your friend? Did I get it all right"?

"Gigi, I didn't mean for all that to happen."

"Little girl, shut them tears up. You knew messing with that boy was wrong, but you just wanted to be down. But I don't blame you. I blame your uncles and godbrothers. How did y'all not notice any of this?"

"She kept shit from us, Gisella. How were we supposed to know?" Kendrick said with a frustrated expression on his face "I've been off the grid for ten years, and y'all just been letting these kids run fucking wild."

"Gigi, I didn't do anything," Eboni blurted out while stuffing her face.

"Eboni, worry about baby number 100 and leave me alone."

"Now, someone explain to me how, why, and when did Kei'sha get in this situation, and what's being done to ensure her safety? And where is Bishop?"

"Gisella, all we know is a man named Eric took her; supposedly, they dated while Kei'sha was in school, but she broke up with him. He has some mental health issues. After Kei'sha and Bishop's wedding, he opened fire on the courthouse steps. Bishop is currently in a comma at Johns Hopkins. We left Tiffany there with his right-hand man, Sincere," Kemetria explained.

"Mablevi and Kendrick, I blame all this on you two. Y'all was out there in the world with them, and y'all was supposed to protect them, make sure they were safe. Now my one and only nephew is hanging on to dear life, and my goddaughter is only God knows where!" I screamed, pissed.

"Gisella, just calm down. You keep referring to them as kids; they are grown-ass men and women. You gotta get that out of your head; when you went away, they were teens and pre-teens," Mablevi added, trying to calm me down.

"I don't give a damn, and where is Moshi?"

"He's back in Baltimore trying to get information on Kei's capture, Gisella we are all trying here. Between the three families, we will get Kei'sha back," he promised, taking out his phone.

"And don't think I forgot you got Trevor in jail playing cops and fucking robbers."

"That issue is being handled. I'm not sure why Lady E would even come down here to discuss that," Mablevi stated with a hint of anger in his voice

"It better be. Now, let's go."

"Go where?" Kendrick asked.

"Back home, it's time I make my presence known again."

Gisella Blanca was back!

Bishop

"Daddy, you gotta wake up and go save them. Mommy is in trouble."

"Who are you, and what do you mean them?"

"I'm BJ. I saved my sister, but daddy, you gotta go get them. That man is hurting mommy. You gotta go back. Daddy, please!"

"Where is she? Who's hurting her? Wait, you called me daddy; BJ, are you, my son?"

"Sorry, daddy, I tried really hard, but when the mean man kicked mommy, I went back to heaven, but my sister is still with mommy. You gotta go save them."

"Wait. BJ, tell me what to do. Why is this happening?"

"Daddy, you really have to go now. I wasn't supposed to come out the gates. Now wake up, Daddy."

"Wait, BJ!"

I was waking up to bright lights and machines beeping all around me. I was dazed and confused.

"Where the fuck am I?" I yelled, trying to adjust my eyes to the lights.

"Good, you're up. I'm Marilyn, your nurse. Let me get your doctor. Your family will be so happy."

"My family?"

"Yeah, they've been waiting for you to wake up every day. They just sit in the waiting room for hours. Let me get them," Marilyn mentioned as she walked out of my hospital room.

When she walked out, I started ripping this shit out of my arm. I felt weak and dizzy, my legs were shaky, and I couldn't stand all the way up. Frustrated, I kicked the table that was next to my bed. My body was in so much fucking pain.

"Sir, you have to give your body time to heal," the doctor demanded, walking into my room and over to help me back in bed.

"Look, doc, give me some pain pills so I can get the fuck out of here?"

"Do you remember anything about your shooting? Do you remember blacking out?"

"Nah, doc, I don't. All I remember is getting married, then feeling a bullet piercing through my chest, and some nut case taking my wife to Cuba."

"Mr. King, I hate to be the one to tell you this, but you were shot multiple times and have been in a comma for a little over three months."

"Three months! Are you fucking serious? My wife is probably lying in a fucking ditch somewhere. Get me the fuck out of here."

"Binky, do you remember me?" A voice I haven't heard from in years asked, walking into my room. There is only one person that ever called me Binky. It was my aunt Gigi, but she abandoned me when my mother died.

"Why are you here? I thought your family didn't want anything to do with me." Now I was pissed, emotional, and in fucking pain, not to mention no one was telling me where the fuck my wife was.

"Binky, I never abandoned you. Who told you that? I've been on the run for years. Just being here is putting my freedom at risk."

"Yeah, well, get the fuck out then. I didn't ask you to be here, and last time I checked, you didn't want anything to do with me."

"Ard, now you are getting a little disrespectful; sit your ass down and listen to me, got damn it!" She raised her voice a little bit.

"You got two minutes; then you can get the fuck out of my room," I hollered, sitting down on the bed.

"I was in your life up until you were about 5, your mother, my sister was killed in a robbery gone wrong. Your shit for brains father got her killed. Even when I wasn't around, I still provided for you. I've always been around, hell who do you think convinced Big Pete to give you a half of brick when you were 15?"

"No, Brian told me my mother died right after I was born and that her family didn't want anything to do with me because I was half white."

"Bishop, that is the furthest from the truth. My name is still on the house y'all lived in. Brian didn't have to work because I was paying for everything. He started stealing again and owed dealers' money, and I refused to keep paying for his fuck ups. Your mother went on a mission with him and was killed in the process. You are a Blanca, always have been, always will be. Your first apartment on Belvedere, I own the building, your first car came from my business partner's dealership. I have always been in your life, and even when I went on the run, I made sure you were good." At this point, she had tears running down her face.

"Everything okay in here?" Another lady came walking into my room with a black pinstripe pant suit on with a white silk blouse unbutton showing her black lace bra and a Gucci purse in her hand. I recognized her from the pictures; this was Kei'sha's mom.

"Where's my wife?" I asked.

"Sorry to be meeting like this, but I'm Kei'sha's mom Kemetria Williams. You can call me Metra."

"Yeah, I've seen pictures of you. Nice meeting you, I guess. Not to be rude, but where is my wife?"

"Bishop, let me get this out the way, I don't do disrespect, and before I let anyone disrespect my family or me, they'll meet my.380," Metra snapped, pulling the .380 out of her purse. "Now that we got that out the way, Gisella is risking her freedom to be here. I don't know what happened to you in the years Gisella was out of your life, but please be clear this woman loves you and has been there since day one."

"How do you two know each other?" I asked, confused as fuck.

"Meechie has been my best friend for a long time. Her husband, Kei'sha's dad, is my right-hand man."

"Wait, you know Kei'sha?

"Kei'sha is my goddaughter."

"Get the fuck out of here," I half-laughed. This was some dateline, soap opera-type shit.

"It's true," Metra interrupted.

"The life I live was never safe to have children of my own. However, I have several godchildren. The Blanca's, Williams, and Knights are all a part of one big family."

"Who the fuck are the Knights? You know what? I could care less. All this isn't bringing me any closer to finding my wife."

"Bishop, I know this is overwhelming and not the right time. However, we will need to discuss your position in the family."

"Position in the family?"

"Yes, you are the only heir to this family. I'm getting old, so you will need to step up and take over. You will now be the leader of the Blanca family."

"I just want my wife; all this other shit will have to wait. Find my Kei' then we will talk about this other shit."

A nigga just wanted his wife not to be Tony fucking Soprano. Damn!

Kei'sha

Eleven weeks, six days, and 23 hours that's how long I've been here. I've been beaten, raped, and verbally abused. Men come and do what they please to me. Mentally I checked out weeks ago. The only thing keeping me alive is the thought of being reunited with Bishop. I wake up to Eric beating me and go to sleep to random men lying on top of me.

"Get up bitch," Eric said, kicking me on my side.

"Eric, please just fucking kill me and get this shit over with."

"Did I tell you to fucking speak to me? Your ass wasn't begging to die when you married that thug. I loved you, and you had the nerve to be with someone you met in jail? Now get up and fix yourself. We have company coming over, and you better play nice. This man is paying me a lot of money for your services, and you better not let me down. Now, go clean yourself up," he ordered, kicking me one more time. Dragging myself out of this dirty-ass bed, I walked to the other side of the room, where Eric kept bottles of water on a broken table. There was a bathroom in this room; however, the chain on my ankle stopped me from

getting to the shower. The furthest I can go is the toilet.

Every day, I thought of ways to kill Eric and the sick bastards

that he invited to have their way with me. Looking at the mirror

in the bathroom, tears ran down my face, my eyes were black

and swollen, there was dried blood on my mouth, and bruises

all over my face, neck, chest, and arms. This one guy liked to

choke me with a belt while assaulting me until I blacked out

then would piss on me to wake me up.

Taking the dirty wash rag, I put some water on it and tried my

hardest to clean myself up. I still had my weave in from when I

got married, so I tried to fix it as best as possible. My stay in

this hell hole was coming to an end. Either I was killing my way

out of here, or I was going die trying. One way or another, I was

getting out of here; I can promise you that.

Tom was the white guy that Eric set up to meet me. I remember

hearing Eric say his name during their conversation. I thought this would be the normal do weird shit to me encounter, but he didn't touch me, just walked around me, sizing me up, then sat with Eric.

"I'll give you $75k for her," Tom said.

"What? She at least worth $150k."

"She probably was until you started drugging and beating her. Look at her damn face, Eric. My girls are of high class, and my clients will not pay for some black junky. Clean her up, and I'll be back in a week," he demanded before getting up to leave.

"Shit!" Eric said, kicking a table. "Come here, Kei'sha, get your ass over here now."

I slowly walked towards him, sitting on the small couch in the front room of this shack. He gripped my neck and pushed me down on the floor; unzipping his pants, he pulled his dick out and shoved it in my mouth, causing me to gag.

"Suck my dick right, you stupid bitch."

"Fuck you, you sick son of a bitch," I yelled after biting his damn dick. He doubled over in pain. I took this opportunity as my chance to get away. I ran to the door, trying to escape, only to find I was surrounded by water and no land in sight.

"You dumb bitch," Eric laughed as he walked towards me. I darted to the side, and Eric fell out the door into the water. I ran to the back of the house and saw a small motorboat docked. Jumping in the boat, I tried to start it up. Before I could get it going, Eric was pulling me out of the boat by my hair.

"I should have killed you a long time ago, you stupid hoe. You will not mess this money up for me."

"Fuck you, Eric, when my husband finds your bitch ass, you're going wish you never were born, clown as weak nigga."

"Your husband?" he laughed. "That half breed wanna be gangster forgot about you already. Do you think he's looking for you? Get real. You were just his little plaything."

"You wish that was the case. Trust me, that nigga coming, and you better have a fucking army on your side with your bitch ass."

"You dumb hoe! We could have been good together, but you just had to marry that thug," Eric shouted, banging me in my face. "Do you know all of what I went through to have you to myself? Kei'sha, I've been loving you since you moved to Baltimore. You don't remember me, do you?"

"Eric, what the fuck are you talking about?" I questioned, holding my bloody lip.

"Kei'sha, I lived next door to you for two years, and you never paid me any attention. All you ever cared about was Nico. Another thug that was no good. I used to watch you give yourself to him every night. Did you know he was married? I had to get him out of the picture, so I killed him."

"Oh my God! you killed Nico, why Eric?" I cried.

"I would do anything for you Kei'sha, you just never noticed me. I followed you to college. When you finally gave me a chance, I thought it was meant to be. But of course, you couldn't love me right; you made me do this. This is all your fault, Kei'sha!" he said, pulling out a gun. "You see, Kei'sha, if I can't have you to myself, I'm making a profit off your ass. Now before I kill your ass, get back in that room!"

Walking slowly back to my jail cell, Eric pistol-whipped me from behind.

"Since you wanna be so hard, Let's see how you do a week without me. Teach you some damn respect," he snapped while walking out the door and leaving me alone.

Six days later...

I sat in this shit hole for days with no clean water or food. I found crumbs of food on the floor to eat and would drink the water from the sink. It didn't matter, though, because everything I ate came back out. Eric got me hooked on suboxone's, but he didn't leave any here when he left six days ago. The first two days were the worst. I threw up extensively, so much that blood started to pour out of my mouth. Then I went through the chills, hallucinations, and weakness. With me going through withdrawals from the suboxone's I was getting weaker with each passing day. This morning, like any other day, I woke up throwing up; rushing to the bathroom, I emptied what little bit of food was in my stomach.

"Aww, is the little hoe having a stomachache," Eric said, walking

into the room with food in his hands.

"Eric, please just let me die. Why are you doing all this?"

"Oh, shut up, here I brought you food, eat up. I'll be back

tonight. Tomorrow is show day." He dumped all the food on the

floor and walked out.

I was so hungry I didn't care that the food was on this dirty

floor. I crawled over to it and ate it all without stopping. With

my stomach full, my mind was clear to think of another escape

plan. I couldn't keep waiting for someone to save me. I was

going save my damn self or die trying.

Bishop

"Bishop, we found her. She's being held in Matanzas; it's right outside of Havana," Metra said as she walked into my room with breakfast in her hand.

"Well, get me the fuck out of this hospital so I can go get my wife."

"It's going take us about a week before we'll have everything set up."

"A week! I've been in this bed for three fucking months, and y'all couldn't have all these families and resources pull together to have shit set up? My wife could be fucking dead in a week!" I was pissed. Here it is, I'm the heir to fucking crime royalty, and these mother fuckers can't get me a fucking boat for another fucking week!

"We have to move strategically to ensure her safe return and that we don't alert the authorities," Metra added, standing next to my bed.

I started pulling shit out of my arm. "I'll go get her, get me the fuck out of here."

"Calm down, Binky." Gisella stepped closer to my bed. She had been sitting in the chair next to me. Gisella was cool for real, my room got switched to a private room, and she had been staying with me every night.

"No disrespect Gisella, but I'm going to get my wife, and can you please stop calling me Binky? I'm a grown-ass man now. Somebody tell me about this nigga that took my wife. I know Kei told me she used to date a lame back in college, said he was on some stalker shit, but she never told me the nigga was bat shit crazy."

"Honestly, you know more than I do. Until you, Kiwi never told me much about her relationships. When she was away in college, she never told me she was seeing anyone.

The only boy I ever know her to date was Nico, and that's because he told me out of respect. I know nothing about this lunatic. Lay or Tiff might know more," Metra stated, sitting down at the edge of my bed.

"I need to holla at them."

"I'll get them on the phone. My husband is waiting for you. Once you are cleared to leave, you will meet him and go over some things. You'll also meet Kei'sha's brother. A few of the guys she grew up with will be going to Cuba with you. We have resources in Florida that will get you guys straight and help get you to Cuba undetected. My son Paul and Gisella have a strong team down in Florida."

"Bet. Where's my phone? I need to call Sin."

"He's right outside. He's been here every day since you slipped into the comma. I'll go get him."

Sin walked in talking on his phone

"Nah, I'll have him call you in a few," Sin said, hanging up.

"Who dat?" I asked him.

"Kei's cousin Lay, she's on her way to your condo."

"Yo, grab my shit. We out of here."

"Mr. King," my doctor said, walking into my room.

"That's not his fucking name," Gisella screamed, scaring all our asses.

"He's a Blanca, and don't fucking forget it," she yelled, stomping out the room.

"Excuse her," Metra said, looking a little embarrassed.

"I understand like I was saying, umm, Mr. Blanca, you had some serious injuries and internal bleeding. I don't think it's a good idea for you to leave."

"Don't care. I'm out. Sin get my shit," I stated, standing up.

"Please, Mr. King, I mean Mr. Blanca, if you are going to leave against my orders, let your body rest and don't do anything strenuous for a couple of weeks. You'll need to sign some paperwork before you leave."

"Got it, doc, Sin, let's get the fuck out of here."

Kei'sha

I made up my mind that tonight would be my last night locked

in this hell hole. When that sick bastard comes back here, I'm

taking his life. The later it got, the more determined I was to kill

this piece of shit. I heard the door open, so I pretended to be

asleep when he walked into the room.

"I wish I didn't have to do this to you. I love you so much. Why

can't you see that?" he whispered in my ear.

"Eric, I don't want to fight with you anymore." I started fake

crying.

"Kei', I'm not falling for that sweet shit. What happened to that

ghetto whore from earlier that was ready to fight?"

"I'm sorry for that. I understand now how much you love me.

Eric, please don't sell me. Can we just start over, just you and

me?" It took everything in my power to say that shit.

"Kei'sha, I wish it was that easy, but it's bigger than you and me.

That man coming back here is the leader of the biggest sex

trafficking rings there is. I can't cross him, and honestly, why would I want to be with you after you've had so many dicks in you?" Eric said, slapping my hand away from his leg. "You really thought you could sweet-talk your way out of this, didn't you? No, you stupid cunt," he blurted out. He got up off the bed and walked towards the door, locking it.

"Now before I sell you, I'm going to have some fun with that phat ass of yours, bend your ass over." With that, he took his belt off his pants, rushing towards me, and snatched me up off the bed.

"Eric, please don't do this." I was crying even harder.

"Shut up!" he screamed. He threw me on my stomach, took his belt, and started beating me with it. "Nah, put that ass up, Kei'sha." Eric was out of breath at this point. This was his thing. He liked to beat me while he jacked off, then he would ejaculate on my ass—sick bastard.

"Yes, I'm almost there, Kei'sha. Shake your ass a little bit, that's right, you lil bitch make daddy come." He was beating me with the buckle of the belt now. I lowered my head and said a silent prayer to God to get me out of this situation.

"UGHHHHHHH, yessss," he screamed as he finished. Laying down on the bed, he smacked my ass and told me to go clean myself.

I tried to move as little as possible. My butt was sore and bleeding from the buckle of the belt ripping through my skin. When I came out of the bathroom, Eric was lying on the bed asleep. I took this opportunity to get the fuck out of here. Eric forgot to lock the leg iron before he passed out. I took the leg iron and stabbed him in his Femoral Artery, and before he could acknowledge the pain in his leg, I got up and sliced his throat. He was dead before he had a chance to wake up. I fished through his pockets to get the key out of his pocket and unlocked the door. Walking around this dirty ass shack, I was determined to get back to my family. We were in a shack on a mountain surrounded by water.

The boat from earlier was docked in the front of the house. I jumped in and started it up. I was about 50 feet away from the house when the shit cut off on me. What the fuck! The bitch

had run out of gas. Fuck!!!

"Mommy, please get up. Mommy, mommy, daddy is on the

way; you just got to get up."

"Wait, who are you? Don't run away, please just tell me your

name."

"Mommy, I'm BJ. We never met. The mean man sent me back to

heaven, but Mr. Nico said, you can do this. He said to tell you to

remember Druid Hill pool. Mommy, I really have to go, but my

sister needs you to be strong mommy."

I had that dream every night. I didn't understand it. I thought I

was hallucinating. Maybe it was a part of me going through

withdrawals. However, tonight's dream was vivid; the little boy

who said his name was BJ looked just like Bishop, just a little

darker. What really stood out to me was the little boy saying,

"My sister needs you to be strong." I never even thought about

being pregnant. Yeah, I had thrown up a couple of times and felt dizzy and weak, but I assumed it was because of the drugs and my current situation. Come to think about it, the whole time I was here, I didn't have a period. As much as I would love to start a family with Bishop, I would die if this baby wasn't his, but BJ said their daddy was coming for me, so I had to think positive. Saving my unborn daughter was now my top priority.

BJ being with Nico brought joy to my heart. I knew he was in great hands. Nico referring to Druid Hill pool brought a smile to my face. The first summer I met Nico, he taught me how to swim. I wanted to go to the gated community pool near my house, but Nico said I needed to learn how to swim in the hood; that way, I'll be able to swim in any kind of water. Getting up off the floor of the boat, I looked around; having no other choice, I jumped in the Cuban waters. I had no idea where I was going, but I started swimming towards the moon. I didn't know how long I was in the water, but my arms started to get tired. I turned on my back, and I started to float to give myself a break. While floating, thoughts of starting a family with Bishop crossed my mind. In less than a year, my life changed so drastically. Besides this whole kidnapping, murdering my kidnapper, swimming to freedom, and being stranded in Cuba, I wouldn't change a thing.

Thinking of my life consumed me, and before I knew it, the sun was coming up. The sun's warmth felt good on my face, I turned over, and I began to swim again. In front of me was a small piece of land. Getting closer, I saw a sign that said Bienvenida a la Habana, Cuba! (Welcome to Havana, Cuba). I walked out of the water, and guards were standing with guns drawn on me.

"Por favor, no dispare. Mi nombre es Keisha Williams, me trajeron aquí en contra de mi voluntad. Soy de América."
(Please, don't shoot. My name is Keisha Williams. I was brought here against my will. I am from America.) I used all the Spanish I knew to get them not to shoot my black ass.
"Ms. Williams, please put your hands up for your safety and ours."

Doing what he asked, I placed my hands over my head

"How did you get here, Ms. Williams?" I'm guessing he was the one in charge because he was the only one talking to me.

"I swam here, but I don't know exactly where I came from. I was being held hostage somewhere."

"Do you know who was holding you hostage?"

"Yes, his name is Eric Stein."

"Was there anyone else there, any other girls?"

"No, just me, can you help me, please? I need to get back to my family."

"Sure, Ms. Williams, I'm Lt. Ares; we will make sure you get to where you are supposed to be."

"Thank you, thank you so much."

"No problem, we will take you to one of our safe houses, and you can clean yourself up, get a good meal, and call your family."

"Great, thank you once again."

"No worries, hey Lt. Braves, come show Ms. Williams where she will be staying."

"I'd love to." I turned my head so fast; it was the guy that came to the cabin. He was a Cuban police officer!

"Ummm, you know what, I'll just call my family and wait for them here," I said nervously. I didn't have a clue what the fuck I was going to do at this point.

"Now, now, now Kei'sha, why would we let you do that?" Lt Braves said in a menacing tone. I turned to try and run, but the other guy grabbed me.

"Listen, la puta; you aren't going anywhere. I have big plans for you; you are going to make me a very rich man. And since you are here by yourself, I'm going to assume you escaped that idiot, Eric. I never liked him anyway. Play nice, and I won't ship your black ass to Bulgaria."

"Please just let me go." I was in tears again. How much more could I possibly take?

"John, take her up to the Cabin and stay there till I can get my buyer down here to pick her up, John don't fuck this up. She's worth more money than you'll see in your life," he said to the guy that was holding me. "And you can go ahead and test the goods," he added, winking at the man he called John.

"Let's go," John demanded as he pulled me by my hair.

"Just let me go, my dad and husband will pay you whatever, just give me a phone, I can call them."

"Just keep walking and shut up," he said as he pushed me into the back of a jeep and drove about 20 minutes before stopping and getting out. Pulling me out of the trunk, we walked up to this abandoned-looking cabin. Inside were three other girls all tied up sitting on the floor.

"The bathroom is in the back. Go clean yourself up, and don't even think about escaping. There's only one way in, and one way out, plus all the windows have been barred," John told me. He then pushed me towards the back of the cabin. I went to the bathroom, turned the water to the shower on, and stepped in. This was the first real shower I had in three months, and although I went from one fucked up situation to another, I was thankful for this shower. While in the shower, the bathroom door opened, a little girl walked in with a towel and some clothes. She looked to be about five years old. I wonder was she being sold too. Seeing her reminded me of the child that was growing in my stomach. I wasn't sure if I was pregnant, but the dreams I had of BJ were so vivid and felt so real. I touched my stomach then continued to shower.

After getting out and drying off, I put the clothes on that was out for me. Surprisingly they weren't too bad, a pair of grey legging and white tank top, no bra or underwear, though. I got dressed, said a prayer, and walked out of the bathroom. I was determined to find a way out of here. Looking into each room as quietly as I could, I saw a phone sitting on this bed, and as soon as I was about to grab it, John came up behind me.

"Now that you are all cleaned up, let's have some fun," he stated, slapping me on my butt.
I couldn't take another man inside of me; I fucking refuse. He was going to die trying to get this pussy.

"I always wanted to fuck some black pussy. Get on the bed now!" John pushed me on the bed and started taking his clothes off. While he was getting undressed, I was looking around for any type of weapon. On the floor next to the bed was a wired hanger. I just needed to get to it.

"Ummm, I-I-I can I have some water first?" I requested, trying to get him out of the room so I can get to the damn hanger.

"Do I look like a waiter to you? You got enough water in the shower, now lay down." John was moving closer towards me on the bed, so I pretended to fall off.

"Are you dumb? Get your black ass back on this bed."

"I-I-I'm sorry." Using my foot to drag the hanger over to me, I slowly got up. As I got up, I put the hanger behind my back and inched back on the bed.

"I heard you got some good snatch. Tom is getting paid top dollar for you, now get over here and show me what's so special about your black ass," he ordered while laying back on the bed. As soon as I got close enough to him, I stuck the hanger hook in his fucking eye.

"Ughhh, you stupid bitch," he screamed, holding his eye. I didn't stop there.

While he was holding his eye, I started whipping his ass; I fought with all my might in that room. I was done with being disrespected, abused, and sexually assaulted. I kept swinging until blood was all over my hands, and John's bitch ass wasn't moving. It took a minute for me to snap out of it, but I finally stopped hitting him and fell to the floor. Looking for the phone I first saw, I grabbed it, and luckily for me, there wasn't any lock code on the phone, but the shit was about to die. Thinking quickly, I dialed my old phone number, but the shit went straight to voicemail. Come on, Kei'sha think. Why would you call your phone? Call Bishop. My hands shook as I dialed Bishop's number.

Bishop

"I bet y'all niggas let me out of this fucking house now," I

hollered, pacing back and forth.

"Yo, Bankz, you just shot me in my fucking pinky toe!" Sin

screamed.

"If y'all don't let me out this fucking house, I'm shooting

everyone, every day, until I get my fucking wife back."

"Bishop, please calm down. We are only trying to do what's best

for you." Metra came into the room, trying to calm me down.

"No disrespect Metra, the best thing y'all can do for me is get

out of my damn house, so I can go get my wife. Y'all sitting here

planning 007 missions and shit. It's been three fucking months.

While I was lying in the fucking hospital, these niggas could have

had all this setup. On some real shit, I'll fucking swim to Cuba if I

have to," I screamed, punching the wall.

"My G, you wilding. Kei' is important to us too, but you going

over there by yourself guns blazing isn't going to bring her back

safely," the nigga Dam added, sparking an L.

"Us sitting here drawing maps and shit like we Dora the fucking the explorer isn't doing shit either."

"Somebody talk to this nigga before I shoot his wanna be badass," Kei's brother Paul said, walking up to me.

"Fuck you, my G, you don't know me, and I could give a fuck less about you. All I want Is my wife. I asked for Dam and Lay; I don't know why all you other niggas even in my face."

"I'm let you have that because you emotional, and you are going hard for my little sister, but hear me clearly, kid, I will kill your bitch ass, and send your body parts piece by piece to every person you love, nephew of Gigi's or not."

"Nigga fuck you and all you're saying. If I don't get to my wife soon, all y'all will be joining me in hell."

"Enough! Paul go sit down; Bishop, let's go," Kei'sha's dad said, standing in my doorway.

"Unless we going to Cuba, fuck we going?"

"Bishop, please take a ride with me, and after I say what I have to say, you can do whatever you want," Kendrick requested, picking up my jacket.

"Bet, y'all niggas be out my crib by the time I come back to."

"Did y'all motherfuckers forget I got shot in my damn pinky

toe?" Sin was sitting on the couch holding his foot.

"Oh, shut your big for nothing ass up, my wife on her way to

patch you up," Paul added as he walked towards the door.

"Is your wife a damn doctor or something?"

"Actually, motherfucker she is," he blurted, walking out of my

condo.

"Bishop, your phone is ringing," Mr. Williams advised as we

were driving around Baltimore. Ignoring him and this fucking

phone, I said, "Mr. Williams, what's up? Why are we riding

around the city like my wife isn't in Cuba with a psycho?"

"Bishop, do you know me? Before you answer, do you know me

outside of what the streets say? Or what Kei'sha told you?"

"Nah, not really."

"Well, son, let me educate you. I started my empire with this

African cat back in the '80s. He had the supply; I provided the

demand. We became a family, his connections became my

connections, and his family became my family. In this life, you gotta have connections, in the drug game, business world, the entertainment world, whatever you are into, you need a connect. Luckily for me, I have a connection for it all."

"I can dig that."

"You are about to become a very powerful man, with any and everything at your disposal. Have you ever heard of Mablevi Knight?"

"Gisella mentioned him, said y'all been working together since the '80s."

"This is true. Gisella and Mablevi are Kei'sha's godparents. This family that you are now a part of is bigger than Baltimore, bigger than Maryland; hell, it's international. Gisella was once the baddest, most notorious Queen Pin in these streets. She used to talk about this nephew she had all the time. One day, she brought you to the park with the rest of the kids, kind of like a play date. That day this clown ass nigga came shooting in the park trying to get at Gisella. After that day, she never brought you back around. Your safety was always her type of priority.

Being her nephew puts you at different tables, in front of different bosses, Bishop not only will you be in charge of the Blanca family, you now sit at the table with six different cartel families. Mablevi Knight introduced Gisella to me back in 82'. After that meeting, the three of us were causing havoc in Mami, New York, and some DMV parts. Mablevi was the first to move to the DMV, and my family followed once I was incarcerated. Gisella stayed in Mami for a while before she went on the run. My son Paul took over my operations when I was incarcerated; he was 15 at the time, so Gisella looked out for him and Keema, that's his wife. They have been together since he was about 13. So, trust me, he gets it when you say Kei' is your life. He would kill for Keema and them kids. Kei'sha, Laylani, and Eboni are all god sisters; Kei'sha and Laylani are first cousins as well. Mablevi inserted himself in Eboni's life without letting it be known he was her godfather. We never wanted our world to disrupt their worlds. I'm telling you all this because you need to know you are no longer in this by yourself. You have the protection and resources from all three of our families, along with the cartels.

Kei'sha is the little sister of some powerful men that will kill Jesus and take his body to God himself for her. And as long as you do right by Kei'sha, they are your brothers as well," Mr. Williams said, hopping on the highway.

"Mr. Williams, I hear you, but I just want my wife. We can do all this meet the family bull shit later." My phone rang for the third time. "Yo, who the fuck is this keep calling me?" I yelled, frustrated.

"Bisshhhop, it's me." The voice on the other end sounded like my Kei' but was scared.

"Kei' baby, is it you for real?"

"That's Kei'sha? Give me the phone." Mr. Williams almost killed us in that damn car, trying to get the phone out of my hands.

"Bishop, please come get me. I'm in Cuba in some cabin. I don't know how long I'll be here. They are trying to sell me.

"What the fuck, Kei'sha? Do you see an address, landmark, anything?"

"All I know is it's near the border of Havana, right at the border were Cuban policemen, but Bishop y'all gotta be careful, the people trying to take me are police officers."

"Kei' who phone is this?"

"I don't know. I found it in a room, and it's on 1% Bishop; please hurry up and get...."

The phone hung up before Kei'sha could finish her sentence.

"Shit!" I screamed. "We gotta get to Cuba now! Kei' said she's going be sold soon," I said, mad as fuck.

"Let me make a call, and we should be able to move tonight," Mr. Williams told me as we continued to drive down I-83, getting off at exit 6 towards Druid Hill/28th street.

"What are we doing here? Didn't you hear me say Kei' needs me now?" I asked as we pulled up to a row house on Lorraine Ave.

"We won't be here long. I need you to meet the DMV crew," he said, opening the door.

When we walked in, there were at least 20 niggas in the living room.

"As y'all know, my oldest daughter has been kidnapped and transported to Cuba. This young man beside me is her husband and will take a seat at the head of this organization. Dam and Kris are well aware and will continue to run the Baltimore/ Maryland region; Bankz will now oversee all other regions."

"Fuck out of here OG, I've been second in command behind Dam and Kris for three years. How this nigga come in and take over? Why because he's sticking dick to your daughter?"

The lil disrespectful nigga said with his chest stuck out.

Boom! Mr. Williams shot the lil nigga in his head.

"Now any other concerns?" he said, putting his gun back in his waist.

"Nah, we good OG," a few others mumbled.

"Bishop, let's go. Y'all niggas clean this shit up and make sure you send him away nicely. Give my nephew the best funeral money can buy."

"Your nephew?" I asked, shocked.

"Yeah, his mother is my daddy's daughter."

"You killed your nephew for being disrespectful?"

"And I'm going to cry at his funeral sitting beside his mother," he said, hunching his shoulders. "One thing we don't do in this family is disrespect, now lets' go. "

The rest of the ride was smooth. Mr. Williams told me a little about the operation. Once we get Kei' back, we would sit down and figure out how to bring my smaller organization into their much bigger organization.

We pulled up to BWI, and Dam, Kris, and Sin were standing at the terminal.

"Fuck y'all niggas going?" I questioned.

"Nigga we going get lil sis, you coming?"

"Say less."

Paul

These niggas were getting on my fucking nerves. Bishop walking round with his bottom lip poked out like that isn't my fucking sister missing. Fuck him being her husband. Then that big ass nigga Sin was on some other shit too. Sorry, y'all, I'm Paul, Kei's big brother. I grew up in Miami with Gisella and my dad's crew when moms moved to Baltimore. I took over the operation fully when I turned 18. It wasn't what I wanted, but by the time I was 18, I had two kids and a wife. I met Keema when I was 13, and she was 14. Keema lived in the group home around the corner from our house.

I met her one night when she had run away from the group home because one of the older boys was trying to touch her. The first night I met her, I knew she was going to be my wife. I used to hide her in our basement every night, and then when everyone was asleep, she would come sleep in my room. I gave her the bed and slept on the floor. We were doing good with hiding until one day, Kei'sha saw her in her one-of-a-kind

Mickey Mouse leather coat. Kei'sha didn't trip or say anything. The next day Kei'sha had clothes on my bed for Keema. I gained so much respect for Kei'sha after that. She was the first person we told Keema was pregnant. On my fourteenth birthday, Keema surprised me by getting us a room at a hotel. Kei'sha helped her set it up and make a cover story of why I would be out all night. My parents knew Keema was my girlfriend, but they didn't know how bad her home life was.

She would stay with me 3 to 4 days out the week and have to go back to the group home so they wouldn't report her as a runaway. The days she was not with me would be the worse. Anyway, on my birthday we lost our virginity to each other. That one night changed our lives forever. Keema found out she was pregnant with my daughter; she was 15, and I was 14. Kei'sha helped us hide it until she was too big to deny it. My dad gave me a job in the organization, and Gisella went and filed paperwork to be her foster mother until she turned 16. Keema gave birth to our daughter Paris two months shy of her 16th birthday, and once she turned 16, she went to court to get

emancipated. That same year I caught my first charge,

attempted murder on this nigga that owed me money. He tried

to play me cause I was a youngin, shot his ass right in the throat.

He lived, but that nigga will never talk again. I ended up getting

five years because I was a minor but got out in 18 months.

When I got out, I stayed with my mom for six months on house

arrest. Keema and Pairs were back in Florida with Gisella. Soon

as I got that shit off my ankle, I moved back down there with my

girl and seed. On Keema's 18th birthday, I proposed to her. Now

we got years in and three kids, two girls Paris and Kennedi, and

one boy Amaru. I put Keema through medical school. She's now

a Nurse Practitioner at the leading pediatric hospital in Southern

Florida. She's on leave right now because of the situation with

Kei'sha. My family is the only family Keema has, so this is

hurting her just as much as any of us.

Honestly, I respect Bishop, but I don't like his ass. All I know is

my sister went missing the day she married his ass and has been gone for three months. I'm not going to hold y'all for too long

just wanted to introduce myself. You'll read more about Keema

and me later on.

Kei'sha

The phone died in the middle of my conversation with Bishop,

but I was confident he would find me. I just have to survive until

then. Looking around the room, I knew I had to do something

with this mess. Somebody was going to come looking for this

dick head. I walked out of the room and started creeping

around the house. There were two bedrooms and a bathroom

back here, in the front of the house, there were one big open

space and a kitchen. Two of the three girls were still chained up

in the front room.

"Do any of y'all speak English?" I asked in a hushed tone.

"We all do. I'm not from Cuba. I came here with my school for

my senior trip. When I went to the local market one morning,

the dude that brought you here grabbed me. The girl over there

has been here the longest; she's dying. The little girl that

brought you clothes is her daughter. She's Tom's daughter as

well," the girl explained.

"Look, I'm getting us out of here, but you gotta help me. I found a phone in one of the bedrooms and was able to call my husband. He's on his way, but I don't know how long it's going to be. We have to make it until he gets here okay," I told her, still looking around to make sure no one is coming.

"How do you expect us to do that? A guard comes here every hour, and according to the clock on that wall, a guard should be here in 30 minutes."

"Shit! Where is the third girl that was here?"

"She in the back with that fat man," she said as I used the key I found in John's pocket to remove the cuffs off of her.

"I'm going in the back and get the other girl. You look for a charger for this phone, find any weapons, money, anything that can help us get the fuck out of here!" I ordered, moving towards the back of the cabin.

In the other bedroom was another man and the girl that was chained when I first got here. I walked in there as quietly as I could. The guy was so focused on what he was doing he never saw me coming. While he was on top of this little girl (she had to be about 16/17 and half his size), I took the lamp off the dresser and broke it across his back. Yelling out in pain, he fell to the side of the girl. She hurried and ran to where I was standing.

"You stupid bitch, I'm going kill your black ass," he cursed, lunging towards me.

I moved to the side, and he fell to the floor. The other girl came running into the room with a charger, three knives, and a thing of bleach.

"Hey, I found this stuff. We should be able to use it," she said, breathing heavy.

"Who's the bitch now, you fat motherfucker! Get your fat ass up and on the bed."

I was sick of this shit, tired of niggas touching me, putting their hands on me, disrespecting me, like I'm not Kei'sha fucking

Williams! When fat ass got on the bed, I had Jessica and Miracle (that's the girl's names) tie him up with the bedsheets.

"Now, you fat bitch open your fucking mouth!" I screamed while pulling his greasy nasty hair.

"You will never get out of this cabin alive," he said, still trying to save face.

"Kei'sha, we do need to hurry this up; another guard will be coming shortly," Miracle pointed out, sounding nervous as hell.

"Open your fucking mouth, and I'm not going say it again!"

He slowly opened his mouth, and I poured the entire bottle of bleach down his throat. "Fat fuck! Let's get out of here," I said, climbing off the bed.

Walking out the room, Jessica picked up the little girl from out the kitchen and some food from the refrigerator "she's coming with us," she said, walking towards the door.

"It's a jeep outside, and I found 10,000 pesos." Miracle started walking towards the jeep.

"Where the fuck can we hide until my husband get here? Once that other guard gets to that cabin, he's going to know somethings up."

I was trying to be calm and collected, but I was freaking out.

"We can go to my family's house; it's in Pinar del Rio, we are about two hours away from there," Jessica said, sitting in the back seat with the little girl whose name was Maria.

"How can we get there undetected? These motherfuckers are cops, I'm sure they'll have everyone looking for us and this jeep," Miracle asked, looking around as I continued to drive.

"This is what we are going to do; we take Central de Cuba towards Calle San Benigno to Route 400, down to Autopista Oeste, then keep going until we get to Artemisa. There are only two gas stations we can stop at without being noticed. I sure hope we can make it with that." Jessica broke down the way to get to her family's house. "Oh, and I found this in the kitchen," she said, handing me a .45 Glock.

"Jessica, you drive since you know your way. I'll sit in the back with Maria."

We pulled over and switched seats as fast as we could.

"Kei'sha, shouldn't you call your husband, let him know what's going on?" I picked up the cell phone and dialed Bishop's number. He picked up on the first ring.

"Kei'sha, we are at the airport now, baby. I'm on my way."

"Bishop, I got out. We are going to Pinar del Rio, Cuba. I don't know how far that is from an airport, but I had to move fast," I said.

"Kei' who the hell is we, and where the fuck is Pinar del Rio? Look to see if that phone you are using is a smartphone?" he asked questions back-to-back.

"Yeah, it's a smartphone; it's an iPhone 4," I said, looking at the phone.

"Kei' go in the settings and turn on the 'Find my iPhone' thingy. Keep that phone on as long as you can. I'll find you Kei', I promise I'll find you." Bishop sounded like he was on the verge of tears.

"Bishop, I love you. Hurry up!" I said, screaming into the phone and hanging up.

The drive took five hours in total because we had to take back roads. We pulled up to this nice size house that sat by itself. Jessica walked up to the house and rang the bell. A lady opened the door and started screaming and jumping up and down. Jessica turned around and waved for us to come inside the house. Jessica's family home was beautiful, and her whole family welcomed us with open arms. I learned that Jessica had been missing for three years. Since she was fucking 13!

"Kei'sha, I want to thank you for helping my daughter get back home. You don't remember me, do you?" Jessica's dad asked. I was trying to remember him, and all I could think was, Lord, please don't let this be another situation I gotta fight my way through.

"No, I don't," I answered with a little attitude.

"I'm Miguel Jose, and I sit at the table with your father."

"Wait, you know my father?"

"Yes, I know him and your godmother, Gisella. I've called both of them."

"You talked to Gisella?" I asked, confused. "No one outside of the family knew that Gisella was still alive."

"The whole table knows Gisella is alive. Your husband Bankz, I think, is what they call him. He's an alright guy?"

"He's one of the realist men I've ever met," I replied with pride.

"Good to know, he's going be sitting at the table soon. Anyway, your father and husband are in Florida. We are going to take my boat to Key West and meet them there. None of you guys need to be boarding planes, trains, or anything that you have to use an ID or passport. Also, those Cuban Police will be taken care of."

"Thank you. I just want to get home to my family."

"I understand. We will leave in an hour," he said, then walked away.

"Hey Miracle, are you staying here or going back with me?"

"Actually, I called my Dad, and he's flying out here to get me, then we are going back home to California."

"Well, if you ever need anything or just want to talk, make sure you call me," I said, tearing up a little bit.

"I will, Kei'sha; thank you so much. If it weren't for you, I would have died in that cabin," Miracle said, wiping tears from her eyes.

We hugged, and I walked towards the boat. It had been a long three, almost four months; I was so tired mentally and physically. I was going home!

Bishop

If I could fly the plane my damn self, I would have been got to Florida. I tell you this; it'll be a cold day in hell before I get on another damn plane. Kei'sha was the only reason I got on this plane. As we were boarding the plane, she called me again. This time we were able to track down her phone. At first, we were flying into Florida than taking a boat to Cuba, but Mr. Williams got a phone call from this guy named Miguel Jose saying that Kei'sha was safe and with him. He was bringing Kei'sha to Key West, FL, and we were meeting him there.

"Who is Miguel Jose?" I asked as we were sitting in this restaurant called Seaside Café at the Mansion.

"Jose is the leader of the Cuban Mafia, you will meet him at another time, but he's a good guy, down to earth, all about his money and family," Mr. Williams replied as he sipped from his water bottle.

Dam, Kris, and Sin were here with us. Gisella was at Paul's house down in Ponte Vedra Beach. The rest of the families were flying down here as well. I talked to and met mostly everyone over the phone. With the exception of Naheem, he was still locked up but was being released as we speak. Gisella made some moves and got him an early release. I knew about him and Trevor from lockup; Naheem was the guy you go to get shit moved around the jail. He was about his money and didn't give a fuck about the politics of the jail. Trevor, I found out was Kei'sha's god sister's husband had got out of jail while I was still in a coma, but he was back home in Baltimore because Eboni had their twins a little early.

I spoke with Kei'sha's cousin Tiffany as well. She was the family's accountant and was good with computers. She helped trace Kei'sha's phone until we got the call from Jose. Thinking about everything that had happened in the last four months, I didn't hear Dam calling my name.

"Bankz's!" Dam screamed.

"Nigga fuck you calling me for?" I said, looking down at my phone.

"He's calling you for me."

I looked up, and there she was, my wife.

"Kei' baby, is that you?" I couldn't believe it. She was standing there right in my face, within arm's reach. When she ran into my arms, I almost lost it. I didn't care that she jumped into my broken arm. All I cared about was that I had my Kei' back.

"Baby, I missed you so much. I was dying out in these streets," I said, kissing all over her face. "Kei' I wanted to come to get you so bad, shorty I was dead out here without you. I was in a coma for three months. I was sick when I woke up, and you weren't by my side." Y'all, a nigga had tears coming down his face.

"Bishop, I missed you so much. You don't know the hell I went through trying to get back to you," Kei' cried as she buried her head in my chest.

"Girl, lift your head. I'm right here, I got you, and you will never go through that shit again, you hear me?" She shook her head yes. "Come on, let's get out of here."

Good Girlz With Hood Habits 2: Welcome Home Kei'

I decided we all needed a vacation before heading back to Baltimore. I figured that a few days in Florida with Paul and his family would be good for Kei'. While we were here, I took advantage of this trip and met the Florida region of my new family's empire. I wanted Kei'sha to go to the doctors, so Keema, Paul's wife, took her to the clinic and did a full physical, and checked Kei' for everything. Sure, enough she was pregnant. Kei' had what they call Vanishing Twin Syndrome. Vanishing Twin Syndrome is when one twin dies in the first trimester because it's so early in the pregnancy. Kei' didn't have to like push it out, or anything, Keema said Kei' or the other baby just absorbed BJ.

Honestly, that was the least of my worries. I was nervous as hell when they ran the test for STDs, HIV, and Syphilis. I love Kei,' but I didn't know if I would be able to handle any shit like that. Luckily all her tests came back negative. Pulling up into the driveway of Paul's house, I was impressed, and it takes a lot to impress me. This nigga lived in Ponte Vedra Beach, Florida. His backyard was the fucking beach. The house was huge. He had nine bedrooms, ten bathrooms, three living rooms, two kitchens, a movie theater, an indoor and outdoor pool, a few maids, and a dope ass car collection.

"Hey Bankz, you and Kei' will have the upstairs area. There's a master bed and bathroom up there, a sitting area, and fresh linen," Keema spoke up as we walked into the foyer.

"Thanks, Keema," I said. I started walking up the stairs to the area Keema said we would be staying. Kei'sha had gone into silent mode right after we got her back. I couldn't get her to talk to me for anything. She still kissed me and hugged me, but that was it, no words were spoken, and I didn't even think about sex. After making sure Kei' was good, I met up with Paul and his crew.

"Sup lil bro?"

"I'm coolin, who you got me meeting?" Paul still wasn't my favorite person, but the nigga was my wife's brother, so I was going to be cool for now.

"I'm just putting you down with the crew, showing you the area and where all the stash houses are. Of course, I'll still be in charge of the Florida operations, but you need to know how the whole operation works. Look, I know we got off of on the wrong foot, but my sister means the world to me, and as long as you treat her right, we good."

"Say less."

We drove from Ponte Vedra Beach to Miami, hitting Daytona Beach, Saint Lucie, and West Palm Beach in between, then back up the coast to Paul's house. Ten fucking hours doing pickups with these slow-ass country niggas. I couldn't wait to get back to my wife. I called the house a few times to make sure she ate and was okay. Kei' had started doing this silent thing and not eating shit. Y'all know I love my Kei,' but that shit was weird to me. Finally, getting back to Paul's house, everyone was downstairs eating.

"Damn, it smells good in here, Keema that you in the kitchen?"

"Don't let this big house and maids fool you. I throw down in this kitchen," she said, bringing Paul and me a plate.

"Where's, Kei?"

"Upstairs watching some damn after-school special," Naheem said, stuffing food in his mouth.

"Did she eat?"

"No, and Bankz, I'm worried. She has to eat or her, and that baby is not going to make it. I tried to talk to her, but she just stares at the damn TV!"

Keema was really worried about Kei'. Shit, we all were, but Keema was taking it really bad.

"I got this," I said, taking my plate upstairs to my wife.

"Kei' come on, bae, you gotta get up and eat." She looked over at me and smiled but still no words. Walking closer to the bed, I sat in the chair beside the bed.

"Do you remember the first time we met?" She shook her head yes with confusion in her eyes. "I always knew you were going be my wife. When you left the jail, I hopped on the Jimmy Mack and called Sin, and I wanted to know everything there was to know about you, from your favorite flower to the type of toothpaste you used." We both laughed.

"Real shit Kei' you are it for me, I can't lose you, and I damn sure can't lose my seed," I said, touching her stomach. "Can you please eat for me, bae?"

With tears in her eyes, she shook her head yes. "By the way, hold on to this for me."

I pulled out a small ring box. Inside was a Platinum 3.41cctw Cushion Cut Halo diamond ring. While I was out with Paul, we stopped at the Mayors Miami International Mall, Paul was there to pick up some money, but I saw this ring and knew I had to get it for Kei'. The ring set me back $50k, but Kei' was worth that and more. Getting closer to Kei' I put the ring on her finger and kissed her hand. After that, Kei' ate everything that was on the plate and fell asleep. I promised Kei' and my unborn child we would get through this. I just hoped that was a promise I could keep.

Kei'sha

I didn't say a word to anyone. I went into my safe place,

watching A Different World from the beginning of the series

until the last episode, then from the last episode until the first

episode. I did that every day the entire time we were in Florida.

"Kei, baby, you good?"

Every day Bishop walked into the room I was staying in and

asked the same question, and every day I gave him a thumbs up

and continued to watch TV.

"Get up and eat."

"Yo lil sis, you still watching this damn after-school special," Paul

asked, walking into my room.

"Nigga leave my wife alone."

"Y'all come on, Kei' still in the bed," Paul screamed.

I looked up, and all these fools came into my room with plates

of food, thank God the room was big. Paul, Dam, Naheem, and

Trevor, sat on the floor at the edge of the bed. Can you imagine four grown-ass men all over 6ft tall sitting on the floor? Lay,

Renz, and Lolo came and got in the bed with me. Luckily it was a

King-sized bed.

"I know one of y'all better move so I can be near my wife."

Bishop was standing on the side of me with no place to sit

"Nigga bring that chair over here and stop whining." Renz was

the first to say something. The two fought like cats and dogs

since the day they met.

"Renz, I swear I'm going to fuck you up."

"Yeah, yeah, whatever nigga take a seat," Lolo said, jumping

into the conversation.

My sisters were sweet and innocent on the outside but were

crazy as hell on the inside. Lauren, a.k.a. Renz, was a beast with

a gun. You wouldn't know you were shot until you were at the

heaven's golden gates. London, a.k.a Lolo, had a thing for fire.

We all found this out the hard way. One day we were at the

mall and saw her little crush walking into Build-A-Bear with another girl. Mind you; I said crush, not her nigga, not her man, side nigga nothing, just a dude she was crushing on. Anyway, Lo asked could we go into Build-A-Bear, never letting us know what was up. We went in there, and this little demon seed walked up to the girl and set her hair on fire and stood there and tried to have a conversation with the girl like she didn't just commit a damn crime.

"Your name Ashley right, you seem like a nice girl, but you need to leave my nigga alone."

She walked away, and the store clerk tried to help that poor little girl out. After that, my mom took Lolo to see a therapist, but after the 2nd session, the therapist quit her practice and moved to Arizona. Lolo said the lady kept asking her was she acting out because someone was touching her, and it pissed her off, so she set her car on fire. After that, my mother just let Lolo be Lolo.

"I swear your sisters going to make me fuck them up, ole fake ass Malibu's Most Wanted," Bishop said, pulling a chair over to the bed and started feeding me. That was the only way I ate.

Nobody could do it. It had to be him; if he weren't around, I wouldn't eat. Bishop was feeding the child growing inside of me, more so me. Being pregnant put me in a bigger depression than being kidnapped, raped, beat, and tortured. At first, I was excited about having Bishop's baby, but then the idea that this baby could be one of those men really fucked me up. Honestly, I started hating the child growing inside of me. Until I had proof that this child was Bishop's, I wouldn't acknowledge it. The little boy in my dream came to me every night assuring me that Bishop was their daddy; however, I didn't believe it. I wanted him to be right. I needed him to be right. If this baby came out to be Eric's or any one of those sick bastards, I was giving it up for adoption.

"The doctor said we could get the DNA test done while the baby was still inside if you wanted," Bishop said, looking down at his phone.

Do you want to know what's so amazing about my husband? Even when I felt unworthy, dirty, and disgusting, the look in his eyes never changed. I feel confident in saying my husband loved every imperfection about me. I just shrugged and went back to watching TV. Maybe if we found out soon enough, I could abort this bastard seed.

"Why all y'all in here getting on my child's nerves?" my mom said, walking into the room. Jumping up and running to her arms, I was crying again. I didn't know she would be here. I thought I wouldn't see her until I got back to Baltimore.

"Auntie, we were just keeping her company dang," Naheem said, walking to give her a kiss.

"Naheem, you put your lips on my wife again. I'm going to put a bullet in your skull then cry at your funeral," my daddy added, mushing Naheem's head away from my mother.

"Damn, Unc, you going do me like that? This family cutthroat. I'm out. Peace."

"Where are you going?" Dam asked, Naheem getting up off the floor.

"Nigga is you my woman? If you must know I'm going to do some site seeing and shopping, you know shit people do in Florida."

"Shut ya corny ass up; I'm coming with you."

"Me too," yelled Renz.

"I wanna go," said Lo.

"No, this isn't no damn field trip," Naheem stated, shaking his head.

I cut the TV off and went into the bathroom. That was my way of telling Naheem I was going with him.

"Well, that settles it, a field trip it is," Lolo said, getting up to go get ready.

"Y'all lucky my sister wants to go, or I'd leave all y'all ass."

"Whatever nigga go get the damn Scooby van," Bishop said.

Walking in the bathroom, Bishop stood near the shower waiting for me to get out. Always there by my side. I just prayed I could get over this and be the woman he fell in love with, and I prayed this baby was his. We all piled in a sprinter and drove 5 hours to Collins St. I can't lie; it felt good to get out of that bed. The sun hitting my face with my husband holding my hand brought peace to my soul.

Bishop went crazy shopping for the baby and me. The damn baby was still the size of a dot and had a wardrobe a grown person would envy. Not only did he buy the child hella clothes, but she/he also had every pair of tennis footlocker had to offer, a Louis Vuitton diaper bag, Gucci this, YSL that, designer, designer, and more designer. Then this fool went and got the same shit for me. I sat back, watching him control the room and run the salespeople crazy. Naheem was pissed we had to keep going back to the van to put bags up. The whole day was just what I needed. When we got back to the house, Bishop ordered all my favorite foods and brought them out back where we all had dinner. Keema was pissed because she cooked every meal we ate and did not like fast food in her house.

"I want to go home," I said, surprising everyone. This was the first thing I said in 10 days.

"Bet, I'll get us flights out tomorrow, Paul said, taking his phone out to book flights.

"No, I want to go tonight."

"Kei, it's 7 pm. I doubt we can do that," my mom spoke up.

"Say less. Pack up we out," Bishop said, getting up from the table.

Touching down, Bishop took me to the condo I brought for him when he first got out. He added some things, but for the most part, everything was still the same.

"Thank you for loving me unconditionally," I said as we sat in the tub.

"Thank you for showing me what love is, Kei. I don't know what I'd do without you. Not only are you my wife, because of you, I have a family now. Not on no weird shit, but I love all them loud ass niggas, including your emotional ass big brother." We laughed, "I have to get used to all this, though."

"We are one big dysfunctional family," I said, chuckling.

Getting out the tub, Bishop lotion me up, pulled out some pajamas he purchased for me, then dressed me. He was so gentle with me, and I truly appreciated it. Sex was not an option at the moment, but the intimacy in just being near him again was enough for me.

"Bishop, what if this baby is not yours? What do we do?"

"Kei' that's my daughter, DNA wouldn't change that. If raising her is too much for you, if she's not mine, I can understand that, but that's my daughter you are carrying. I wanna show you something."

He reached for my hand, then walked me down the hall to one of the extra bedrooms. We didn't know for sure if the baby was a girl or boy, but Bishop was set on it being a girl. Opening the door, I was greeted with a Pink, yellow, and white themed room with Bri'annna written on the wall. He had a crib, full-size bed, changing table, rocking chair, and two dressers in the room. Both dressers were filled with clothes, along with the closet. On the wall, there were pictures of everyone in our big ass family with their relationship to Bri'annna written next to it. Bishop had a big ass TV mounted on the wall as if the child would be watching this big ass TV, a PlayStation, X-box, and iPad on the shelf under the TV.

"Bishop, why are there game systems in here?"

"I didn't know what type of toys to get her. I mean shit, I never had a kid before."

"Really, bae," I laughed. "Where did you get the name

Bri'annna from?"

"I was watching Princess and the frog one day; I liked the name

the lil black girl had but wanted to put a B in it."

"When did you ever watch Princess and the frog?"

"You know, in the jail niggas can only watch DVDs and the news.

A CO brought that shit in one day, and that name always stuck

with me."

"I got her a whole bunch of Disney movies too, but I want us to

watch them first to make sure it isn't no weird shit going on."

I walked over to the DVD collection, and it had to be 100-200

DVDs in here.

"Bishop, I'm not watching all of them movies. When did you

have time to do all this? And who's to say we are having a girl?

What if it's a boy?"

"Kei' trust me, it's a girl, but just in case it's not, the room on

the other side of the bathroom is decorated just like this except

its gray, blue, and yellow and has Bishop Jr. on the walls instead of Bri'annna. I had people working on these rooms while we were in Florida. They redid the whole condo."

"Bishop, I love it, and I love you. I know you want this baby. I just don't know, bae," I cried.

"You remember on the plane when you were telling me about the dreams you were having about a little boy," Bishop asked, standing behind me with his arms wrapped around my waist.

"You mean BJ?" I questioned.

"I didn't tell you, but I had the same dreams. I didn't want you to think a nigga was crazy or anything."

"I didn't know that."

"You see, that's how I know this baby you carrying is mine. I promise you she is. I know you feel disconnected from her because you think she's not mine. Baby, I promise you she is."

"I'm so scared, Bishop; what if I can't take care of her? So much of her will remind me of what happened to me."

"Kei, I promise you once you see that little girl looking like you, you won't remember the negativity around her."

I sure hope he was right.

6 ½ months later

"I swear to God, Bishop; I'm never having another one of your big-headed kids ever again! UGHHHHH," I screamed as another contraction came.

"Girl, shut up. You going have ten of my babies, then we're getting a puppy."

"I'm never touching you again!"

"Okay, Ms. Williams," the doctor started to speak.

"Hey, nigga I have done told you her name is Mrs. Blanca!"

Yeah, just to feel you in, Bishop legally changed his name to his mother's last name.

"I-I-I'm sorry." The doctor was terrified; Bishop had been screaming at these people for two days. Yes, I was in labor for two fucking days, and this stubborn little girl did not want to make her damn exit, and if she didn't come out soon, I was reaching in myself and pulling her out.

"Mrs. Blanca, it's time to push. On my count, I want you to push for ten, then breathe. Got it?"

"Got it. I'm ready."

"Alright, 3,2,1 push."

"UGGHHHH!" I screamed.

"That's good. I see her head. Alright, give me one more good push."

"I can't, please, just let me rest. Bishop on God, I hate you."

He just laughed and got down next to the doctor and started talking to our daughter.

"Hey, lil momma, don't be messing up my pussy with that big ass head. If it doesn't snap back, you going to grow up without a father."

"Bishop, get the fuck away from me," I yelled.

"She's out!" the doctor screamed like he was the damn daddy.

"I knew that would work," Bishop said, smirking.

"Wah wah wah," my daughter was crying, and her father was about to die.

"Give me my damn child." When the doctor passed me my baby, I fell in love with her automatically.

"Bishop, you lied to me."

"Huh, what I do?"

"You said she would look just like me. This baby looks like you spit her out. Ugh, I really don't like you now."

"Kei, well, I did put in all the work."

"Bishop!"

"What it's true."

"Just go call the damn family."

"We going get put out if all them niggas come up here."

Bishop walked out to call everyone, and I had some one-on-one time with my new baby. Holding Ms. Bri'annna Gabriella Blanca was truly amazing.

"Man, just get your ass up and come see your niece. Bishop was hanging up the phone."

"Who was that?"

"Dam ass talking about why we were calling him so early in the morning, nigga it's 11:13 am."

"You know, Dam, don't get up till 2 pm."

"Well, everyone else is on their way. Moms said we should have called her when you first went into labor. She also said she's going to kill me for telling security not to let anyone up for visits."

I busted out laughing; Bishop told security no one could visit me until after the baby was born.

"This the second time someone told me they were going to kill me in one day. I'm scared now," he said, laughing.

A few hours later, my room was filled with people, gifts, food, and music. Gisella went back into hiding after I was returned home. She moved to Mexico this time, so she wasn't here with us, but she did call and got me placed in a private suite so we could have more room. I've been coming to Johns Hopkins for years and never knew they had private rooms.

"Bishop, I'm getting tired," I told my husband.

"Ard, I got you, babes. Y'all niggas gotta go."

"Bishop!"

"Oh, my bad, excuse me, my wife is tired and wants y'all to leave."

"I'm so glad my parents left already; you are so damn rude."

"Man, let me say bye to my niece and get out of here before I shoot ole rude ass over there," Naheem said, getting up from the couch he was sitting in.

"Why this family so damn violent."

"Why you so rude?" I asked.

Everyone walked out, saying their goodbyes and sending love. Bishop picked up Bri'annna and walked over to my bed.

"You know when you're ready, I want like nine more, right?"

Smiling, I put my head down. Having more kids was a touchy subject for me. Since getting back home, I still haven't healed totally. Physically yeah, I'm good, but mentally it's some things I still haven't gotten over, like sex.

"Kei', don't do that. Put your head up, ma, don't ever feel ashamed about what happened to you. I'm here, your nigga isn't going nowhere, and neither is this dick."

"Bish, I'm sorry, it's just I know you have needs and are still young. What if I never want to have sex again?"

"Then I guess you better buy some more of those fruity-smelling lotions so I can make me a fefe."

"Really, man, you are crazy."

"Crazy bout mine now; kiss me and go to sleep. I'm holding Bri a little longer."

"You know you can send her to the nursey and get some sleep."

"Hell no, I'm not sending my child down there so some lonely overweight miserable nurse can steal my child, yeah ard."

"No more Lifetime for you, sir," I said, turning over to get some rest.

Bishop

I can't believe I'm a father. My daughter is beautiful, and her mother is amazing. I couldn't wait to have more kids. I wanted at least ten more. We were in a good spot right now. My wife was home and getting better every day, my baby girl was born and healthy, and my business was booming. It's been about three months since Bri'annna was born, and it was time to get back to work.

"You ready for this meeting?" Sin asked as we sat in the rental truck. We were in Mexicali, Mexico, a small city next to Tijuana, Mexico. This meeting was supposed to introduce me to the other families at the table. I was also meeting my grandfather for the first time that I can remember. Mr. Williams, Mr. Knight, and Gisella would be here with me to make sure everything goes smoothly. Gisella was back in hiding, so we had to fly into San Diego, CA, then took a cab to Tijuana's airport to meet up with Mr. Williams. He flew straight into Tijuana then we rented a truck to drive 2hrs and 30 minutes to Mexicali, Mexico.

"Them niggas bleed just like I do, fuck I need to get ready for? I tell you one more thing; I'm tired of fucking taking flights and driving to these off-the-grid places."

"Man, me and you both feel like I'm Dora the exploring or some shit. Let's get this shit over with," Sin said, getting out of the car.

Walking into this business meeting Bishop went to sleep, and ruthless Bankz woke up. We walked into this big ass warehouse to sit down with the other five families in this cartel. Although I was with family, I don't know all these niggas, and I had to keep my head on a swivel.

"Welcome, gentleman. As you know, this is Kendrick Williams, Gisella Blanca, and I am Mablevi Knight, Bishop; it's nice meeting you. I've been brought up to date on everything that has been going on. I just want to say welcome to the family, and I'm sorry for what happened to Kei'sha."

"Appreciate it," I said, keeping it light. We were here to discuss business, not talk about my family.

"Bishop, the purpose of this meeting is to introduce you to all the families and their Lt's. I'm assuming Sin will be your Lt. Over the next few weeks, you will also sit with our legal business partners and have the businesses transferred to your name." Gisella was explaining to me while taking us on a tour of the warehouse.

"Now, this warehouse is for the guns and weapons of our operation. We transport from this warehouse by boat, never in vehicles. Once the shipment gets to the individual drop-off points, it is up to the LT. of each region to get to the pickup point within 30 minutes. We keep a tight timeslot with all drops offs, pickups, and money collections. The warehouse back in Baltimore near the Port is the only warehouse that product comes through for the DMV region. We have two drop-off days per month. You and Sin will be the only ones to know those dates, and they switch every month. Besides those two days, no one is allowed in this warehouse as far as workers.

Workers are given an hour's notice when to report, and if they can't make it, they have to wait until the next month to work.

Each worker gets paid in cash after their shift. There are three shifts, and the first shift is for the chemist. They come in to mix, cook, and cut the product. An hour later, the next shift comes in. These are your packers. They bag up everything and separate each order by state, city/county, block. Your last shift is your driver's. Now it's more of them than your regular works. Your drivers work like a track meet. One driver picks it up, drives about three or four blocks from here, switch cars and driver. The next driver drives to the block it's going to or to the next drop-off point. That all depends on where the product is going. If the product is going out of Maryland, there are six drop-off points before reaching the final destination. Once all drivers make it to their endpoint, they make a call, and their payment will be placed in their family's mailboxes. All drivers have to have a permanent place of residency and at least one family member they love. Just in case they decide to steal or snitch, we will kill their family. Chemist gets paid $10k each shift, your packers get paid $5k each shift, your Maryland drivers get paid $7k a shift, VA drivers get $5k, and DC drivers get $8500. We do a pay increase once a year. Once a worker has been here for

five years, we give them a retirement package and let them go."

Mr. Williams laid down the breakdown of how the drug and gun

operation worked, and the shit was mind-blowing. My

operation back in Baltimore was child's play compared to this

shit.

"You have full range to change things as you see fit. This is your

operation now, Bishop," Mr. Knight said, walking up behind me.

"I want to introduce you to my son."

"I know this not the nigga that got lil sis going up in a frenzy." I

turned around, and it was my nigga Moshi.

"Get the fuck out of here, this black ass nigga your son? No

wonder y'all need me," we both laughed.

"How do y'all know each other?" Mr. Knight asked.

"Pops, that's my nigga from K-section. He's the one that helped

me out in that little situation I was in back in the day."

"You mean when that big ass nigga was about to stick a dick in

you in the shower, and your ass was screaming like a bitch

losing her virginity," I said, laughing even harder.

"Oh, nigga you got jokes, you know damn well that's not how that shit went down."

"Nah, I'm fucking with you. What's up, my guy?"

"I can't call it, so you're my boss now," he said, chuckling.

"Something like that."

"Well, if you going be the leader of anything, we gotta get you out of these Kiddie disco clothes."

"Nigga fuck you; I'm cooling. I'm leaving all that pretty boy shit to your black ass."

"Come, Bishop, you need to meet the rest of the operation. You and Moshi can talk later."

"Ard bet, I'll get up with you later," I stated, giving Moshi dap.

"Bet, we're hitting this little club tonight; come through," Moshi said before leaving.

Walking towards the back of the warehouse, I saw a big ass table with about ten niggas sitting down and at least 50 more standing up.

"Why are we even giving him a seat at this table? The Blanca family is doing just fine with the leadership it has. We already have the Williams and Knights sharing in with the Blanca's. I don't see why anything needs to change." One of the dudes sitting down was talking mad disrespectful.

"Steve, are you questioning me?" My grandfather Alejandro Blanca asked as he sat at the head of the table.

"Of course not. I'm just making sure you aren't making a big mistake and turning your empire over to some new half breed," the prink responded, turning beet red.

"Well, to be honest, I don't want the damn empire, could care less about it. But since my grandfather asked me to take it over, and I plan on putting hella babies up in his daughter," I said, pointing to Mr. Williams. "Not to mention my Auntie over there wants me to take this empire to another level I figure why not," I said, sitting next to my grandfather. "Now, Steve, you can either shut the fuck up and keep your position at this table, or you can die right now your choice," I stated, putting my feet up on the table. Steve got up to walk out.

"I will not be disrespected by this half breed," he responded with his crew following him. They never made it out of the warehouse. Like my father-in-law said, this family don't do disrespect. Fuck him and his crew.

"Kei'sha, you not putting no holes in my daughter's ear. You can chill with that shit," I said, getting dressed to go meet up with Moshi at the club he told me about earlier.

"Bishop, it's nothing wrong with getting her ears pierced. All little girls get it done as a baby."

"Not my child, then you want to take her to a mall and get some cheap ass earrings, nope not happening. I'll be home tomorrow; we can take her to the jewelers and get them done. Fuck I look like having my daughter wearing some $69.99 earrings." We fussed through facetime every night I was away, which seemed to be often nowadays.

"What club you're going to, and when you start dressing like Jay-Z in the '90s," Kei'sha joked with her face all in the camera.

"Moshi brought me this damn shirt. He said it's Versace or some shit, you know me, I'm a polo type nigga."

"Yeah, ard, don't make me come to Mexico and fuck shit up."

"Girl, you know this dick belongs to you and only you." We continued talking until Sin came knocking on the door. "Ard Kei' I'm out, let me see my baby girl real quick." She showed me Bri'annna lying next to her in a onesie and some pink socks. "Why you got my daughter in them cheap ass clothes?" "Bishop, get off my phone. What she supposed to sleep in?" She hung up on me.

Me and Kei' never really argue, but when it comes to my daughter, I'm always going to go overboard. I hate when Kei' puts her in cheap clothes. I could wear the same sweatpants three days out of the week but my daughter, she going get the best of the best and can't nobody change my mind. When Kei' wasn't around, I threw her dirty clothes away and brought more.

The club Moshi invited us to was some hole-in-the-wall club, 20 minutes away from where we were staying. The vibe was cool, but I'm not a club-type nigga, and Sin looked like a fucking giant in here next to all these damn gwulla gwulla niggas. I wasn't

staying long; I just wanted to show my face and kick it with my

homie. Moshi came over to the section we had and brought

some thick as Spanish women with him. One girl caught my eye.

She was darker than the rest of the women, tall, thick, and had

hazel green eyes, kind of reminded me of that model chick,

Bernice. She was fine, but my Kei' looked better. Moving away

from the crowd, I sat back in the booth and started looking at

pictures in my phone of my girls.

"Why you sitting here by yourself." The chic that caught my eye

came over and sat next to me.

"Why you in my personal space?" I answered nonchalantly,

moving further away from her.

"Come on now. I don't bite," she said, moving closer to me.

"Unless you want me to." Oh, she was bold. I'm not going to lie.

I was kind of intrigued.

"How bout we take this party back to my hotel room," she

suggested, getting close to me again, this time sitting in my lap.

"No disrespect, but get the fuck off me," I said, pushing her up off me.

"Well, if you decide to change your mind, here's my number."

She handed me a card with her name and phone number, I took it to be nice, but I knew I wasn't going to use it. As much as I liked her style, I loved my wife and daughter too much to fuck up. I stood up and walked to the bathroom across from my section. On my way to the bathroom, I texted Kei' to let her know I loved her and couldn't wait to get back home to her and our daughter. Washing my hands, I heard the door open, looking up it was shorty.

"I'm assuming you are married. That's why you turned me down. Well, I can keep a secret if you can," she said, getting closer and closer to me. My brain was telling me to move, but my feet were stuck. What the fuck was going on?

"Nah, I don't do secrets," I said, trying to remain cool.

"Well, how bout I keep the secret, and you go home and tell wifey about all the freaky things I did to you." At this point, she had her breast against my chest and her lips on my ear, licking

my damn ear with her hands going down to my pants. I couldn't

stop her for some strange reason like I knew I needed to move,

but my body wasn't listening.

"I see someone is happy to see me," she said, squatting down

and unbuckling my pants. Her mouth was on the tip of my dick

when someone busted through the door.

"Sorry, I didn't know anyone was in here. I can leave," a man

stated, looking at me and shorty.

"Nah, you good, my G." I put my dick back in my pants and

damn near ran out of the bathroom. I can't believe I even

allowed a bitch to get that close to me. Shit! Walking to our

section, I told Sin we had to go, left 5-$100 bills on the table,

and rolled out. Let me get my ass back to Baltimore before I

ended up in divorce court.

"Yo, the shit not funny nigga. What am I supposed to tell Kei'?" I

asked Sin as we were on the plane to go back home.

"My G, nothing happened. You said the girl barely had the tip of your shit in her mouth before the nigga walked in. Why would you tell her anything?"

"Sin, I've never lied to my wife, and after all Kei' been through, I'm not trying to fuck our shit up." I was nervous as fuck after last night.

"Bankz, you think too much, calm down and forget about that shit. You sound like a lil bitch for real," Sin said, turning his headphones on and leaving me to my thoughts. I was going tell Kei'. I couldn't keep this shit from her.

Kei'sha

While Bishop was away in Mexico, I had a meeting with Lay, Tiff, and my mom. Lay's dad left her a little over a million dollars, and she wanted to invest it in something. My mom and Tiff did all the books for our family.

"So, Auntie, what can you do with this money before I blow it all?" Lay asked, turning her phone face down on the table. I noticed she's been real sneaky lately, which means she was fucking with some ain't shit nigga that was going to use her sooner or later. But I'm letting her live for now.

"Well, first, Laylani, we are going to put some of your money in a CD. You're going to do an 18-month term with a locked-in rate. Then we are going to invest in real estate. I have a few agents you can work with. I suggest you get two or three rental properties. Also, I'm flying out to California at the end of this month to look into the cannabis industry; you should look into investing into that as well," my mom said, pulling out her iPad to show Lay some information.

"I trust you, auntie, whatever you say, I'll do it. I made you an authorized user on my account so you can get everything started."

"Kiwi, have you checked on your investments? I know the house on Biddle St. needs some work done, along with the house on Eden St."

"I know. I got contractors going over there next week. I've been so busy with Bri' Bri', and Bishop, and I haven't had the chance to get over there," I responded, taking a sip of my water. "I'll check in on it. Tiffany, were you able to change everything over to Bishop's name?"

Everything except the restaurant, because of the liquor license, it has to stay in Uncle K's name until we can get the liquor license transferred as well. And Kei'sha, I put all the Rita's in your name using your maiden's name," Tiffany explained.

While I was away at UMES, Tiff got her MBA from MSU. She opened her financial firm, and the Blanca, Williams, and Knight families were her only customers. She cleaned money, made our investments, kept the books for all the legal businesses, and was everyone's financial advisor. My mom went back to school and got her CPA license, and worked with Tiff part-time.

"Well, ladies, I have a date with my husband, so I'm going to go ahead and leave, but lunch is on me," my mom said, getting up and leaving $300 on the table.

"Now that she's gone, I need to tell y'all something, and I don't want y'all to start acting crazy," Lay whispered once my mom was gone.

"What you do, Lay?" I asked, sitting up in my chair.

"If you started messing with Si again, I'm going beat your ass myself," Tiff said, irritated already.

"See, this why I didn't want to tell y'all anything," she said, sucking her teeth.

"Fuck that; let me get Eboni on the phone so that she can hear this too." I picked up my phone and face-timed Eboni.

"What up Kei'?" Eboni said, sounding like she was asleep.

"Your best friend said she has something to tell us, so I wanted you to be on the phone when she told us so you can cuss her out too," I spoke into the phone.

"Oh, lord! Lay what you do now?" Eboni questioned.

"Y'all hoes make me sick. I didn't do anything wrong. I was just going to tell y'all GM is out, and he called me, and before y'all say anything, no, I'm not getting back with him. I think he knows I put Lamar on his block, and I wanted to ask Kei' if she could get me one of Bankz's guns," Lay told us all in one breath.

"Lay, what do you mean you gave Lamar his block?" Eboni said, now sitting straight up, more focused on the conversation.

"I mean, I took money from GM along with some drugs from his connect and gave Lamar his corner up by Dutch village. The nigga played with my heart, so I played with his money."

"I think you have lost your damn mind," Tiffany, who was quiet the whole time, said.

"Do you even know how to shoot Laylani? Are you ready to catch a body? What about your kids? You need to find out what he knows, and then we will move forward, but none of our husbands are getting in the middle of this shit. Lolo and Renz

will help you with this. And the next time you wanna play billy

badass, do me a favor and don't!" I spoke up before, getting up

and walking out of the damn restaurant.

"Eboni, can you believe this shit? I swear that girl is missing a

few screws."

I was pissed. Lay, always act of emotion, never logic.

"Just have the twins go meet up with that nigga, don't even let

Lay know, just end that nigga lease and keep it pushing. Did you

notice she didn't mention if he asked about his daughter or

not?"

"Yeah, I peeped that. The nigga only worried about pussy and

using her ass."

"Right!"

"I'm hit up the twins and get this situation handled asap."

"Bet. Call me later. I'm going back to sleep."

"Hoe, where all the kids?"

"School, with their aunt, and with Trevor, I got this house to myself, and I'm enjoying the silence," Eboni said, hanging up on me.

I pulled up to my house and was shocked to see my husband's car in the driveway.

"Bishop, you here?" I yelled, walking into the condo.

"Yeah, I'm in Bri' Bri' room. Why she not here, and where you been?" he asked before I could get to the damn room.

"Well, hello to you too, she's with my sisters. Why?"

"Kei'sha, you got my daughter with your gun-toting, firebug ass sisters?" he yelled.

"First of all, you need to calm down and stop all that screaming, and Bri'annna usually stays with her gun-toting mother and father, so what's the difference?"

"Whatever, man," he said with a little attitude, walking away from me.

"Bankz!"

"Now Kei' you know, you don't call me that."

"I know my husband Bishop isn't standing in front of me, so I must be looking at Bankz. Now you want to tell me what the fuck is going on?"

"Kei', you know I love you right, and I would never do anything to hurt you on purpose?"

"Yeah, I know that. What's wrong?" He was starting to scare me a little.

"Nothing's wrong, so look, when we were in Mexico, we went to this bar, and this girl brushed up on me and was like about to suck my dick, but I stopped her." Bishop looked like he was about to cry.

"Fuck you tell me this shit for Bankz. It's cool, I'm not giving any up, and you got needs. It's cool."

"Kei' come on now, it's not like that, and it didn't even go that far."

"I said it's cool. I'm about to head out. I'll see you later." I let go of his hand and walked towards the front door.

"Yo Kei, come on, it's not that serious. We can talk about this shit. I swear nothing happened." His words fell on death's ears.

Getting in my car, I drove aimlessly for a while, just thinking. Did I believe my husband? Yeah, but I still was pissed and hurt. The fact that a bitch got that close to him was fucking with me. I ended up going over to my mother's house since that's where Bri' Bri was at. Bishop called and texted, but I refused to answer the phone. At first, I was going to tell my mom what was going on, but I figured it was no need because I was going back home to my husband, and there was no need to bring others into our drama. Around 3 am I walked into my home with my daughter. Putting her down in her crib, I walked back into the kitchen and took out the biggest pot we had. I filled it up with ice and cold water. I walked into the room I shared with my husband, and I dumped the entire pot on his ass.

"What the fuck," he screamed, jumping up out of bed.

"The next time, it's going be boiling water. Don't ever in your life play with me. I don't care if nothing happened. She shouldn't even got the chance to get that close with your simple ass." I threw the pot at his head and walked out of the room. I heard it hit the wall; he must have ducked. That night I slept in my daughter's room and prayed this was the first- and last-time temptations would test my marriage.

"Bishop, if you call me one more, I promise you I'm getting a divorce." I hung up on him. This was the third time he called since I've been out of the house. We still weren't on the best terms, I mostly ignored him, and he tried his hardest to get me to talk to him. It's been about a week since he came back from Mexico, and all he did was buy me stuff and apologize. Honestly, he was wearing me down, but I refused to let him know that.

"Come on, Bri 'Bri' let's get this over with so we can get back home before I kill your father."

We were here to get her ears pierced, finally. Bishop wanted to get her VVS yellow diamonds. I tried to convince him there was no point in spending all that money on her first pair of earrings, but he wasn't feeling it.

"Damn, she's beautiful," some guy said, walking up behind me.

"Thank you," I said, being nice.

"Maybe her mom will let me take both of them to lunch."

"Nah, son, keep it moving."

We both turned to see Sin towering over the guy.

"My bad big man." The guy walked away.

"Sin, what are you doing here?"

"Came to make sure my goddaughter was good. Why you got these cheap ass clothes on her?" he questioned, taking Bri'annna out of my hands with a little attitude.

"It's nothing wrong with Baby Gap Sin. Did Bishop send you here?"

"Nah, I was with my shorty when I saw cornball trying to mack. Fuck he was in your face for Keidi?"

Keidi is what Sin called me. I have no idea why so don't ask.

"Your shorty? When you start going out in public with chicks?" I asked. Sin never, and I mean never was seen out in public with any woman that wasn't family.

"Don't worry about me, Keidi, worry about if that nigga you were talking to will live to see tomorrow."

"The man came up to me 5 seconds before you. What did you want me to do? Shoot him for talking to me."

"Right in his fucking dome. I'm taking Bri' to Nordstrom's; we'll meet you back in the food court in an hour."

"Sin, don't buy her another damn piece of clothes. I swear I'll fight you, and she's cranky because she just got her ears pierced."

"Girl, back up, I got my fat momma. Come on, Breezy, so we can get you out of these cheap ass clothes. I bet your da-da don't know she put this ugly shit on you," he said, talking to Bri' like she knew what he was saying.

He walked away, leaving me standing in the middle of the damn mall by myself. I walked and sat down in one of those massage chairs. I put a $5 bill in it and closed my eyes. Feeling the vibration and pressure going down my back woke something up in me I haven't felt in a year. I jumped up because I damn near had an orgasm in the fucking chair. Reaching for my phone, I sent my husband a text even though he was still on my shit list.

Me: meet me at the house in an hour.

My World: What's wrong?

Me: Just be at the damn house in an hour, damn!

My World: Say less.

I called Sin and asked could he watch Bri' for the rest of the day.
He agreed to keep her till tomorrow. Sin had a nursey put
together the day Bishop asked him to be Bri'annna's Godfather.
She literally had a room and everyone's house. Even Eboni and
Trevor had a room for her, and they have six damn kids.

I made a beeline to Victoria's Secret and picked up something
sexy to put on; it was time to remind Bishop why he fell in love
with me. Rushing to the condo, I took a hoe bath and shaved as
quickly as possible without cutting my damn self. When I got
out of the bathroom, I lotion myself down, went into Bishop's
private weed stash, rolled him up a blunt, and walked down the
steps to meet him at the door. I decided to ditch the lingerie

and stood at the door naked. I heard Bishop turning the doorknob.

"Man, don't be having none of your hoes around my daughter."

I couldn't hear Sin's response, but Bishop hung up the phone as soon as he saw me.

"Damn Kei' this how are you coming?"

"I haven't even begun to cum yet. Let's go."

Walking back to our room, I undressed Bishop and made him lay on the bed.

"Here, I passed him the blunt I rolled. Smoke it while I handle him," I demanded, pointing to his hard dick.

"Kei, baby, no doubt I'm happy as hell, but I don't want you doing anything you don't want to because of what happened in Mexico."

Instead of talking, I took my tongue and licked the shaft of his dick, licking the head as well, making sure to get all the pre-cum that oozed out of it.

"Shhhhh Kei, baby, that feel so good."

I lowered my mouth over his shaft. I made sure my mouth was wet. Bishop's dick was touching the back of my throat, causing me to gag a little. I forgot how big this motherfucker was. Taking my left hand and placing it on his dick, I started sucking and jerking him off at the same time, making his shit wet and sloppy.

"Fuck, Kei, yes damn do that shit, you nasty bitch."

I loved hearing Bishop call me a bitch while I was giving him head. It made me super wet. I started going faster and faster using both hands now.

"Kei, I'm about to cum."

"Cum right in my mouth, daddy."

"Oh, my godddddd," Bishop screamed like a damn banshee.

After I was done pleasing my man orally, I laid down next to him and just listened to his heartbeat.

"Oh no, get that ass up, come take this ride."

"I was giving your old ass a chance to catch your breath."

"Oh really, my old ass huh, say less."

Before I knew it, Bishop was up and gripping my ankles.

"I'm going to show you old, spread them legs."

This man put my legs on his shoulders, lifting my bottom half off the bed and bringing my pussy to his lips.

"Bishop, what are you doing?" I got no response, at least not in a verbal way.

Bishop started kissing my thighs and the outside of my cat, pausing to blow on it.

"Damn, that feels so good."

Flicking his tongue over my clit, Bishop was teasing me. He kept sucking on my clit, then stopping, taking his finger and putting it in me, then taking it out.

"Bishop, if you don't stop playing with me, I'm going to kill you."

"Damn so violent. I got you, babe hold on."

With that said, he dived his head in my creamy middle, not stopping until I came multiple times and begging him to stop.

"Baby, please stop, oh my god, please, I can't take it, put me down."

"What you say? Didn't you call me old?"

Good Girlz With Hood Habits 2: Welcome Home Kei'

"I'm sorry, Bishop, damn."

He let my legs down, and I tried to slow my breathing down when this man flipped me over and spread my checks. Thinking he was about to enter me, I prepared for the pain, but oh no, he stuck his tongue down the crack of my ass. Rubbing my cheeks as he made love to my ass with his mouth. It felt so damn good. I never had this done before, hell how did Bishop know about this? Oh, shit, do that again, I thought to myself as he put his finger in my hole while licking around it. I felt a trembling in my stomach I never felt.

"Bishop, something not right, my body feels so crazy."

"Just let it go, Kei," he said, applying more pressure.

"OH, MY GODDDDDD," I screamed as I came so hard my body felt weak and had I been standing up, I'm sure I would have fallen. After that, I blacked out.

"Kei, baby, you good?"

I woke up to Bishop standing over top of me with a glass of water in his hand.

"Yeah, I'm good," I replied sluggishly. Damn, it felt like I was drunk or something.

"How long I've been out?"

"About 30 minutes. I put a hurting on that lil cat, huh. And you didn't even get the dick yet."

"Bishop, where did you learn how to do all that stuff?"

"Porn Hub and Red Tube."

"You sure that's all?"

"Kei', don't do that; you know this dick belongs to your ass. Now get up and ride this motherfucker so I can go to sleep."

"You sure about that?"

"Kei, don't do that. I told you nothing happened with that damn girl."

"Calm down. I was just joking, now sit back and enjoy this ride, old man."

Good Girlz With Hood Habits 2: Welcome Home Kei'

Bishop

The last few months have been crazy. Between this new operation, reconnecting with my family, my daughter, and my wife, a nigga was losing it. I was flying out every week damn near to get this business the way I like it. The workers were solid, and it wasn't much I needed to change, but the operation was larger than I expected. In the last six months alone, I've traveled to New York, California, Mexico, Florida, Jersey, and South Dakota. Like who the fuck sells drugs in South Dakota. It was a lot, and my wife was not the biggest fan of my world tour. "Yo, Dam, your sister is going kill me if I'm late for this photoshoot," I said as we were sitting in the warehouse.

Kei' set up this photoshoot when Bri' was six months but I had to go out of town, so she rescheduled it to today, and if I missed it, I mine as well pack my shit. We were cool now, but every time I pack my suitcase, her little eyes started to roll, and the attitude followed.

"Man, that's Sin big ass over there caking up on the phone with his shorty."

"Man fuck you, ain't nobody caking. I just made one phone call. This nigga be on the phone all day every day with Kei,' and nobody says anything, but the minute I make one phone call, it's a problem," Sin said, catching a little attitude.

"Yoo, this bitch must be special. She got you going to bat for her," I joked. Sin never shows interest in a bitch besides smashing.

"Don't call Lay a bitch!" he barked.

"Nigga did you say Lay as in Laylani Williams as in Kei'sha's cousin/godsister?"

"Bankz, I swear if you tell your wife, I promise you, I'm shooting your half breed ass."

"Yeah, whatever, you just better do right by her, or Kei'sha will have your ass."

"That's what I want to talk to y'all about. Lay got this nut as ex by the name of GM. The nigga just got out and been in Lay ass on some; you owe me money shit. Bankz, I need you to get some intel on the nigga for me," Sin explained.

"How you wanna do this?" I asked, ready to go to war for my family.

"I want the nigga brought to me alive. I'll let my Goodie handle his bitch ass," Sin requested, standing up.

"Who the fuck is Goodie," me and Dam asked at the same time.

"Lay, damn! That's what I call her. Just get the shit done," Sin said, walking out the warehouse. I got my ass up and left too. Let me get my ass to this photoshoot before my wife kills me.

"I can't believe this shit," I heard Kei'sha saying coming from the bathroom in our room. I had just walked in from another trip and was dead tired. I heard Kei' and Lay talking, so instead of screaming her name, I got quiet and just listened.

"Bitch, you just like Eboni fertile ass," I heard Lay say as I stood in the doorway of our bedroom.

"Shut up. I'm not ready for another child yet. Bri'annna just turned one. My husband is in and out of the state like he's a damn flight attendant and has a whole drug empire he's running. I would be damn near a single mother with two kids. Nope, I'm not keeping this one," Kei'sha spoke like a person I never even met.

"Now you know Bishop is not having that shit."

"What Bishop doesn't know won't hurt him," Kei' replied, walking out the bedroom and smack dap into me.

"Now I'm going to pretend I didn't hear you talking about killing my seed," I said, looking at her like she was the scum of the Earth.

"Bisssshop, I don't think we are ready for another baby just yet. We can try again in a year," she suggested, looking scared and nervous.

"Kei, if you kill my seed, that's the end of us. On some real shit." I told her as serious as I could be. I promise you as much as I love Kei' killing my seed was not an option.

"Bishop, can you please turn the music down? I'm trying to put Bri'annna down for her nap."

"Are you going to talk to me about my baby you are trying to kill?" I questioned as I sipped my double shot of Hennessy.

"Can we skip the dramatics' today, Bishop damn!"

"Kei' on some real shit, you got me fucked up. How you get to decide what happens to my child without talking with me?" I was pissed at this point.

"Bishop, we have a daughter that barely sees you, three days out the week you on a world tour, then when you are in town, you're either at the warehouse, the club, or one of the other fucking businesses you own. I'm not raising another kid by myself."

"By yourself, by your fucking self Kei' how you sound? All the shit I do is for you and Bri'annna, and you think I give two fucks about this empire? I will give this shit up and move to a fucking farm with you and ten fucking kids! You the one on some selfish shit. Man, fuck this, I'm out." I grabbed my jacket and left out. I rode around for a while then ended up on Baltimore Street. By now, I was drunk and pissed the fuck off. I stepped into the 2 o'clock club and got a VIP section.

"Yo, Bankz, what are you doing out in these streets?" My nigga fat Norm walked up to my section with a bad-looking shorty on his arm.

"Shit, I'm trying to get like you," I said, slurring my words.

"Where your friends at, lil momma?" I was really feeling myself cause I don't even talk like that.

"Bankz, how about you come with me upstairs to the private room." Some light skin shorty with a fat ass said, grabbing my hand.

"Fuck yeah," I responded, slapping her ass as she walked in front of me.

Before I could get to the room, I was slapped on the back of my neck.

"What the fuck?" I said, turning around, ready to shoot a motherfucker.

"You lucky I didn't shoot your ass, fuck you doing here, Bankz?" I looked up, and it was Paul's big emotional ass.

"Ask your damn sister why I'm here. She wanna be killing babies and shit."

"Bankz, get your ass up and go home."

"After I get my dick wet, maybe I'll get this chick pregnant.

You'll keep my baby, wouldn't you?" I was talking reckless at

this point, but I didn't give a fuck. I changed for Kei'sha, and she

wanted to kill my seed because a nigga had to work?

"Nigga, get the fuck up and go home."

"Paul, fuck you, my G."

"Bet. Hey shorty, put the word out nobody dances with this

nigga, or I'm killing everybody in here," Paul said, lifting his shirt

to show his .45.

"Cockblocking ass nigga, I'm out." I got up, smacking the bitch

on her ass again and walking out. It was 3 am when I got home.

I laid on the couch and was knocked out.

Waking up to the house phone ringing, I looked at my cellphone

and saw it was 9 am. Bri' and Kei' was gone already, and I

wondered why they were up and out so early. Answering the

phone, I was shocked and pissed.

"Hi, this is Dauphine calling from Planned Parenthood to

confirm an 11:30 am appointment with Kei'sha Williams."

This sneaky selfish-ass wife of mine!

Kei'sha

I made an appointment to get rid of this kid as fast as I got it. He wasn't leaving me, so I wasn't worried about his little threat. It's crazy the minute I started fucking again, I get pregnant; it has to be Bishop. I've never had any pregnancy scares before him, and now I'm just popping out babies like I was a damn factory.

I walked into the Planned Parenthood on Howard St and was surprised to see it empty. "Hi, I have an 11:30 appointment to terminate a pregnancy."

"Now, I didn't believe it when the clinic called to confirm the appointment. I said I know my wife didn't go behind my back after I told her ass I would leave her if she tried to kill my seed."

"Bishop, what are you doing here?"

"No, the question is, what the fuck are you doing here?"

"Babe, just listen. I didn't think we were ready for another baby just yet."

"So instead of talking to your husband, you decide to handle this on your own?"

"Bishop, you are never home, I'm not working, and I just didn't want us to get in over our heads."

"Kei'sha miss me with that bull shit. We are not hurting for shit, you could stay home for the rest of your fucking life and have 20 kids, and we still wouldn't be hurting for anything. The shit you just pulled was selfish."

"Bishop, can we just talk about this at home?"

"Nah, Kei'sha, you can go head to your condo. Me and my daughter don't need you."

"The fuck you just say, Bishop?"

"It's Bankz, only my bitch calls me Bishop, and you lost me the day you decided to kill my kid. I'm out."

"Bishop, Bishop, I tried to run behind him, but he got in his car and left."

I called his phone but got the operator telling me the number has been changed. Hopping in my car, I drove straight to our place, and he wasn't there. I called Sin, and Sin didn't answer either. Crying and not wanting to go home, I went to my mother's house.

"Have you lost your damn mind, little girl? You killing babies now?"

"Ma, please, I didn't kill the baby; I was just scared."

"So, scared you couldn't talk to your husband?"

"I don't know, ma, I wasn't thinking."

"Clearly!"

"Well, since you know all that, do you know where Bishop and Bri'annna at?"

"Yeah, he came by and picked her up and said they were going to Disney World for a few days."

"What, he took my daughter out of the state? Oh, hell no, I'm going to the airport." I said, getting up out the chair I was sitting in and stormed out of my mother's house.

I know I was wrong but damn, you just going kidnap my damn daughter. When I got to the airport, I lied and told the ticket lady my daughter left her asthma pump, and I needed to give it to her father. She printed me out a boarding pass, and I went through security, looking at every gate for Bishop and Bri'annna.

"Mommy," I heard Bri'annna calling my name.

"Hey baby girl, you and daddy leaving mommy?"

"Kei'sha don't make a scene in here. When we get back, I'll bring her to you."

"So that's it, Bishop. Just like that, you're done with me."

"I can't trust you, Kei'sha. You could have come to me about anything, but you chose to be sneaky and conniving."

"Bishop, please let's go home and talk about it."

"Nah, me and baby girl going to Disney, catch you later."

He picked Bri'annna up and said, "Oh, by the way, hold on to this for me."

He placed his wedding band in my hand.

"I won't be needing that anymore. We out. Peace."

He walked away with Bri'annna in his hand and my heart in the other. Bishop left me. My world was over. I never thought we would be here. I was scared and thinking irrational. How could one bad judgment call ruin everything?

Good Girlz With Hood Habits 2: Welcome Home Kei'

It's been three weeks since Bishop walked away from me. He and Bri'annna were still in Florida. He only called my mother and father. He did send them pictures which they sent to me; other than that, I hadn't seen my baby girl or my husband. When I left the airport, I went to a hotel. I didn't want to be in any of the houses if my husband and kid weren't there. The only reason I kept my phone on was just in case Bishop called me. He never did. As week four slowly rolled around, I decided to get out of my room and go to the hotel indoor pool. Maybe the water would make me feel better. It did until a group of badass kids came in splashing and making too much noise. I left and went back to my room. In front of my room door was a yellow envelope addressed to me. I assumed it was my bill from the hotel, but to my surprise, it was court papers. Bishop was requesting a divorce and full custody of Bri'annna. What the fuck?

Bishop

"Shut up and just suck my dick before my daughter wakes up, damn."

I was ready to send this bitch home. Leaving Kei' never crossed my mind, I thought we would be together forever, but she killed my seed. After all, we have been through; she took it upon herself to make a decision that would affect both of us. So, I left. I took my daughter and went on a little vacation. Y'all remember the chick from the strip club in the private room, that Paul bitch ass was cockblocking, well that's who was here sucking my dick. I know, bad decision, and I'm sure I'm going to pay for it later on, but right now, I didn't give a fuck. Every night I would have her come to my room and suck my dick while Bri'annna was sleep. I never fucked; there was no kissing, hugging nothing, she never even saw my daughter. I took all my frustration out on her face then sent her on her way with a couple of bands.

"Bankz, I'm not about to keep sucking your dick and not getting fucked. Where they do that at?" Nicole said.

"You lucky, you even here lil mama, now either do what I asked or get out, it's that simple." I was getting annoyed at this point.

"Fine, but I'm not going keep pleasing you, and you not return the favor," she said, all the while taking my dick out and doing what she was here for.

Little did she know this was the end for her anyway. Tomorrow we were going home, and I was going to talk to my wife. I sent her divorce papers yesterday. I wasn't for sure I was going to go through with it. I was just pissed and hurt.

We got back to Baltimore about 6ish. I took Bri'annna to Kei'sha parents' house. I had Nicole get an Uber to her house so Bri'annna wouldn't see her ass. I texted her once I dropped Bri off to tell her I would bring her bags to her house.

"Come in for a minute," Nicole requested, touching my hand.

"Nah, I got some shit I need to handle." I was done with her ass.

She served her purpose.

"Well, help me with my bags," she begged, rolling her eyes.

"Ard."

"You want some water?"

"Yeah, that's cool, I said, walking out of her bedroom after

putting the last bag in her closet. Drinking the water, I sat down

on her couch and started drifting off. Either she put something

in my drink, or I was really tired. I woke up the next day to my

phone blowing up.

"Sin, what's good, bro?"

"Nigga where you been? Your wife on IG acting crazy."

"Fuck, you mean? What she doing? Showing her ass or

something?"

"Nah, lil sis down bad, I think she bout to do something crazy.

You need to get to the Marriott downtown asap."

"Say less." I hung up and rushed to my car. I needed to get to

my fucking wife.

Kei'sha

"Well, that's the end of Bishop and Kei'sha," I said, drunk in the camera. I was on my Instagram Live drunk, not giving a fuck. "Can y'all believe this nigga left me and took my kid? After everything I've been through, he just ups and leaves me. Talking about, I can't trust you," I mocked in the camera. I had 1700 viewers watching me self-destruct. "But the nigga was down Mexico getting head from some taco-eating hoe!"

Mom0f6: Kei, come on now, what are you doing?

MoneymakingLay: Wya, Kei', let us come get you

DamDaDon: Lil sis get off this shit and call Bankz

"Fuck Bankz, I screamed! He out in Florida fucking Minnie Mouse. I never did wrong; I upgraded his fucking life, and this is what I get. He could have left me in fucking Cuba if he was going hurt me like this"

Zone18Sin: Kei'sha, come on lil sis, y'all going get past this

"Nah, I'm over this shit. He doesn't want me. He is taking my daughter away from me, probably with the next bitch right now. Is that why you left? You wanted new pussy, yeah that's it, fuck you Bankz and that bitch!" I said, pulling a .38 from under my pillow. My blood is on y'all hands. Kiss my daughter for me. I lifted the gun to my temple. The safety was already off. I cocked it back and was ready to meet my son finally.

Boom!

Before I could pull the trigger, Bishop came busting the door down.

"Kei' what the fuck are you on?" he asked, walking towards me on the bed.

"Leave me the fuck alone," I said, pointing the gun at him. I was now enraged.

"Y'all pussy's going tell him but ain't stop him when he took my daughter or wouldn't let me see her," I screamed back into my IG Live. "I hate all y'all."

"Kei' baby, give me the gun."

"Oh, now I'm Kei' baby? Was I that when you sent me divorce papers? No, get out of here and let me die in fucking peace."

"Kei' I'm sorry I overreacted, but you taking your life isn't going to solve anything. Baby, please, I promise we can get past the shit."

"Nah, I'm out. Peace ain't that what you said when you walked away from me?" I said, putting the gun back to my head. This time Bishop tackled me. He got the gun out of my hand.

"I hate you, I screamed in his chest. Why would you do this to me? Get off me!"

"Kei' you just tried to kill yourself twice, and on fucking Instagram at that, I'm not going nowhere."

"Yeah, you are. I don't want you, Bishop. You hurt me in the worse way. I didn't even go through with it, damn."

"So, you were going kill yourself, knowing you were still carrying my seed."

"Fuck you and your seed nigga." I said as I wiggled my way from under Bishop. I walked over to the table that the papers were lying on, picked up a pen, and signed them.

"I thought I would be with you forever. I was ready to kill myself over you leaving me. When you kicked that door in just now, I thought what we had could be saved. That was until I smelled you. You really wanted to be with another bitch that bad, Bankz? You smell like that cheap ass, Love Spell, and before you fix your lips to lie to me, your bitch left a hickey on your neck. Damn, here I was ready to die for you and you out here living for the next bitch," I said, shaking my head.

Walking to the door, I stopped and looked back at the love of my life. "I know I need to get help because I never really dealt with what happened to me in Cuba, but today just confirmed we should have never been together. I'm going away for a while. I'll be back for my daughter." I walked out the door and felt dead inside.

1 year later

Bankz

I'm going to kill him and his whole fucking family, I thought as I sat in my car and watched this lame bury his face in my wife. The nigga wasn't even doing the shit right. It's been a year since Kei' left me, and I be damn if I didn't miss her like crazy. The first three months she was gone, I was freaking off with any bitch that would suck my dick. I never fucked; no bitch could ever say they fucked me besides my wife. I still had Nicole hanging around, but the shit with her was getting boring. Around month four without Kei' I started drinking more and even started popping pills. It wasn't until Bri'annna found my stash of pills that I got my shit together.

Six months after Kei' had been gone, I started stalking her ass. I wanted my wife back. We both fucked up, and it was time to get our shit back tight. The nigga that was about to die name was Lance. He lived on the floor above Kei' in her new apartment. His pressed ass was trying to get with Kei' even when she was pregnant. Yeah, she kept my baby, and we had another little girl. Kei' thought no one knew about the baby since she moved upstate to New York. I know everything about my wife. I was even in the hospital when she gave birth. I brought the building she was living in. Every time she paid rent, it went to an account for our daughters. Soon as Kei' was ready to come home, I was selling this building but not before putting Lance out on his ass.

Kei'sha

When I left Bishop in that room, I left with nothing. I realized

how bad I was mentally that day. While I was living and loving

my husband and daughter, I wasn't loving myself. I decided I

needed to leave to get better. I didn't want to leave Bri'annna,

but I knew she was in good hands.

"Hey, babe, where you want me to put the bags?"

"Lance, I've told you multiple times stop calling me that."

"My bad, Kei'."

"Don't call me that either."

Lance lived in the apartment above me. I moved into a 2-

bedroom apartment in Long Island, New York. I've been here for

about a year now. I talk to Bri'annna every day, but I haven't

seen her or Bishop since I left. From what I hear, he's been

causing havoc all up and down the DMV. My brother told me he

shot a McDonald's worker in his pinky toe because they didn't

have the toy Bri'annna wanted. After my suicide attempt, I

started seeing a therapist twice a week. It was hard at first to open up to her, but after a while, I did, and it was just what I needed.

"When you going to stop playing with me and be my girl?"

"I'm not playing, we are friends, and that's it."

"I wasn't your friend when I had that juice box in my mouth, now was I."

Rolling my eyes, I walked away from his clown ass. I let this nigga taste my shit here and there when I was horny, and the vibrator I had wasn't cutting it. His head game was nothing special, so I don't know why he was bragging about that shit.

"Look, my daughter bout to wake up. You can just leave my shit at the door. Thank you."

Yep, I had the baby that I was going to abort. Kei'anna Gisella Blanca was the spitting image of me, and she was a chunky little thing. No one knew about her. I never spoke about the baby, and when anyone would ask, I'd change the subject.

"You know I got my step daddy degree."

"You also got four kids by three different women. I'll pass."

"Damn you heartless, whatever kid, I'm gone. One."

I was so glad he left. Little did he know this would be the last time he saw me. I was going home.

Two weeks later:

Walking up to Bishop's condo, I was a little nervous. I mean, how would you feel if your ex knocked on your door with a baby in her hands? When the door opened, I was surprised to see a woman on the other side.

"Can I help you?" she asked with an attitude.

"Is Bishop here?"

"Who the fuck are you?"

"Nicole, why the fuck are you answering my door?"

"Bankz, who is this bitch?" she said, pointing at me.

Bishop looked down at me and smiled.

"Bitch you know who this is, and you know what time it is. Get out."

"What you mean get out? How are you going put me out over this weak ass bitch?"

Before I knew it, Bishop slapped the girl he called Nicole.

"Trick, I told you the day my wife came home, it was a wrap for you, now get out."

I stood there shocked, confused, and a little turned on, to be honest.

"Kei' get in here with my daughter. It's cold as shit out there."

Bishop took Kei'anna's car seat and shut the door in the girl's face.

"Look at Daddy's baby, Kei', get over here and kiss your nigga."

"I'm not kissing you; I don't know what you and lil momma were doing."

"The bitch was sucking my dick, but that's about it."

"Bishop!"

"What Kei' she was, damn. I didn't smash, though. Only pussy that's been blessed with this dick is yours."

"You want me to believe you ain't fuck none of the bitches I heard about?"

"Not one, a bitch may have played with my kids in her throat, but I ain't stick my dick in none of them."

"Yeah, whatever, sir."

"Damn Kei' I missed you. Come here. Damn, you look sexier than ever."

He picked me up and spun me around. Damn, I missed his touch. Just his hug had a bitch ready to bust it wide open for a real nigga.

"Bishop, we need to talk."

"Kei' wait, let me say my piece really quick. Look, I know I overreacted about the abortion. There's no excuse for that. I also know I wasn't truthful with you either, the day you and Lay were in the house, and you found out about the pregnancy, I was pissed, but I figured we would talk about it later. When you never said anything to me, I felt like a bitch. But the last straw was when the clinic called to confirm your appointment. I guess you forgot you gave them the house number, and I just happened to be home. Kei' I felt like a failure. Like damn, my bitch didn't think I could take care of her and my seeds. The night before your appointment, I went to a strip club and was about to do some wild shit in private with the shorty you just saw. Luckily Paul was in town and stopped me."

I stood up, ready to leave.

"Chill Kei' let me finish. When I saw you at the clinic, I wanted to hurt you as bad as you hurt me. I took Nicole with me to Florida."

"You had her around my daughter?"

"Not on no caking shit, I promise Kei', she stayed in a different room on another floor. The bitch was annoying. To be honest, I ain't stick no dick in her, but as I said, she did suck my dick. We came back to town the night before your suicide attempt. I dropped Bri' off and made the mistake of going over to her house. I swear I didn't fuck shorty, I wanted to, but my dick wouldn't even jump when shorty bent over with her ass in the air. She sucked my dick, and I fell asleep. I woke up the next morning to Sin blowing my phone up, saying you were geeking on Instagram. I thought you were shaking ass or something. I would never have thought you would try to kill yourself.

I never wanted to be the cause of so much pain. Kei, she put that fucking hickey on my neck while I was sleep. When you left the hotel, I was down bad. I started drinking, smoking harder, and popping pills, a nigga couldn't look at me wrong or I was killing him and his whole family. I let your mom keep Bri' till I got myself together. Kei' I fucked up, babe. I'm sorry," he explained with a tear rolling down his face.

"So, the bitch on the other side of that door that's kicking and screaming like a damn child don't mean shit to you?"

"Fuck no! She was a wet mouth, that's it."

"Bet, kill her."

"Say less."

Bishop walked over to the bookshelf that held his safe with his .45 in it. He took the safety off and walked to the door.

"Shorty, my bitch said it's up for you," he said, aiming the gun to her head.

"Bishop! You are really going kill me."

"Fuck yeah, if my wife doesn't fuck with you, fuck, I look like letting you breathe her air."

Before he pulled the trigger, I stopped him.

"Bishop, that's enough. Put the gun away."

"You sure, babe?"

"Yes, crazy-ass."

"Crazy bout mine, always. Kei, am I getting some pussy tonight?" he asked while closing the door on the girl's face.

"She's going be a problem," I told him.

"And I'll be the fucking problem solver. Come on, let's go get Bri' so she can see her sister."

"How did you know?"

"Know what?"

"When you first saw me, you said bring me, my daughter. How did you know I kept the baby, and it was a girl?"

"Kei, if I could find out all your information and locations while I was in jail, do you think it would be hard to find out now? Oh, and that nigga Lance, dead that before I do."

"Bishop, it's nothing too dead. I do want to be honest with you."

"I know you let him suck on my pussy. He lucky I didn't kill his ass already. The only thing that saved him is how unsatisfied you looked when he was down there. Nigga can't eat pussy for shit. I'm cool on yo long as he didn't stick no dick in you, we good."

"Bishop! You were watching me?"

"Told you I'm crazy bout mine. I wanted to scoop you up so many times, but mom dukes were like you needed to heal. So, I stayed in the background, watching you become strong again. Kei' not for nothing a nigga really love your ass. Now let's go get baby girl."

Walking into my mother's house seemed a little weird. How do you say, hey, mom, sorry I been gone a year but here's another grandchild?

"Bitch, you were pulling a Meredith Gray on us?" Renz said, coming down the steps.

"Shut up, fool," I responded, hugging her. "Where everybody at?"

"In the basement, Daddy got a new TV and is insisting everyone come down there to watch it."

"Oh Lord, let me go and get this over with."

"SURPRISE!!!!" everyone screamed when we walked into the basement.

"Oh my God, when did, how did y'all do all this so fast?"

"This nigga had us on standby every day since you gave birth thinking you were coming back," Dam mentioned.

"Nigga shut up," Bishop said, standing behind me holding my waist.

"Kei'sha, if you ever pull a stunt like that again, I will kill you then cry at your funeral," my dad said, walking over to hug me.

"Well, damn, I thought he only threatened me. Glad he's an equal opportunity killer," Naheem said, laughing. "Look, lil sis, I'm glad you're back. Please stop disappearing. I got to go. Here this is for Kei'anna." He handed me a thick envelope and left.

"Lil sis, please don't leave this nigga like that again. I thought the nigga was going to shoot my other pinky toe with his ole emotional thug ass. We out, but this is for my goddaughters." He also handed me a thick envelope. "Come on y'all," Sin stated. Lay, HC, and Lay's daughter Brooklyn got up and walked over.

"Bae, why are we leaving so early?"

"Bae? When did y'all get together?"

"When you were in New York entertaining lames," Sin joked.

"Man, go to hell. You better not hurt my cousin Sin."

"Shit, she be abusing me, tell her don't hurt me."

"Shut your ass up," Lay said, playfully slapping Sin.

"Kei' I'll call you later," she stated, giving me a hug before heading to the steps to leave.

"Nah, call her tomorrow. She'll be getting dicked down tonight."

"Bishop!" Me, my mom, and Lay screamed.

"Oh, my bad," he said, walking deeper into the basement.

"Where Eboni and Trevor?"

"At the hospital, one of the kids had an asthma attack. She got too many to remember their names," mom responded, taking Kei'anna out of my hands. "So, you decided to come back home, huh?"

"Kemetria, don't start that shit, my daughter ain't been here ten damn minutes, and you are acting up," my dad screamed from the other side of the basement.

"Kendrick ain't nobody acting up. I was just asking a question."

"Well, clearly, she decided to come back home. Isn't she standing in front of you?"

"Ard now, Kendrick, don't get fucked up in front of these kids now."

"Woman, hush, the only person going be doing the fucking up around here is me when I get you upstairs."

"Ard, now y'all come on with the grandparent's porn. Shit almost made me throw up," Bishop said, pretending to gag.

"Bishop, shut your ass up, like you and my daughter, don't be fooling around."

"Your daughter be taking advantage of me. I'm innocent."

We all busted out laughing.

"Y'all a trip, mom where Bri'?"

"Paul came and got her a few hours ago. Paul took her on their Uncle/Niece date he does every time he's down here."

"Can you call him and see how long they are going to be? I'm going to feed Kei'anna upstairs. Thanks, everyone, for being there for Bishop and me while we were going through this storm. It really means a lot to me."

"Cuz, you know we got you. Come on, Mosh," my cousin Tiff said.

"So, while I was away, all you niggas just started fucking with my family? Mosh, how you pull square ass, Tiffany?" I asked, surprised to see them together.

"She saw the numbers in my account and couldn't resist a nigga," he said, winking his eye.

"Yeah, whatever nigga," I chucked, walking up the steps. I went into the room Bri' had here and fed, changed, and put Kei'anna down for a nap. I didn't realize I dosed off too until I heard Bri'annna talking.

"BJ, this our little sister. Okay, BJ, I'll protect her. Love you too."

"Bri'," I called out.

"Mommy! Look, we got a baby. BJ said it's my sister, and I have to protect her as he protects me."

"Bri' come here, let mommy talk to you."

"Okay, mommy."

"Bri' I know we talked to you about your brother BJ, but you do know he's in heaven right, he's not here to talk to you."

"Mommy, I know that he's in heaven with your friend Nico. And BJ said I could talk to him all the time because God put him in my heart."

The tears just started to fall from my eyes.

"Mommy, don't cry. BJ always says to be a good girl and not make you cry because you have been hurt a lot, Mommy do I hurt you?"

"No, never, Bri'. You could never hurt mommy."

"Good, I can't wait for my sister to meet my brothers, so I can teach her how to protect them as BJ taught me."

"Bri' you only have one brother in heaven."

"BJ said I got two more brothers coming," she told me, jumping off my lap running towards her daddy.

Oh, hell no, I thought. Not two more come on, God, do it really gotta be two?

"Babe, you ready to go home?" Bishop asked, licking his lips.

Shaking my head, I walked out of the room, turning the light off. This nigga is going keep me barefoot and pregnant.

"Kei'sha, I'm not wearing no fucking condom to fuck my wife."

"Bishop, you heard what I said. I'm not getting pregnant any time soon."

"I swear I'll pull out, but Kei' for real how a three-year-old got you scared like that?"

"BJ is up there working on something with him and God, I feel it.

Shit, every time you touch me, I get pregnant; nope, no, sir. You

want lotion or baby oil," I said, laughing.

"Ouch, why you throw that damn pillow at me, Bishop?"

"Do I want oil or lotion?" he mocked. "You really testing me,

Kei'. As a matter of fact, come here right quick."

"Nah, I'm not fucking with you in Target."

"For real, Kei' come here. I wanna show you something really

quick," he said, gripping my hand leading me to the family

restroom at the front of the store.

"I swear, Bishop, if you try anything, I'm going to scream."

"That's my plan, make you scream my name," he said, locking

the door.

"Bend that ass over Kei'."

Doing what my husband asked of me, I put the palm of my

hands on the sink and arched my back. Bishop lifted my skirt up

around my waist.

"How are you going tell me I can't feel this pussy raw when she creams for daddy, and I ain't even touch her yet?" Bishop was standing behind me, staring at me in the mirror.

I was so damn hot. I never fucked in a public place before. This shit was new and exciting.

"Tell me what to do, Kei'," Bishop said while biting my neck.

"Put him in Bishop."

"Who's him, Kei'? You gotta use your big girl words." Bishop was sliding his dick up and down my slit, applying a little pressure but not putting that big motherfucker in me.

"I want you to put that big ass dick inside of me now, Bishop, please."

"But I don't have a condom," he said, placing his finger on my clit.

"Bishop, just fuck me damn it!"

"Say less."

He slid his dick in my wetness, and for a minute, we just stood there looking at each other in the mirror. God, I love this man.

He started to move; at first, I kept up with his strokes, but this man was on demon time.

"Shit, Bishop, oh my god, yes fuck me." I tried not to be too loud, but he was hitting my spot.

"Now, what were you saying about condoms?"

"Nothing Bishop, nothing oh my god, yes, baby right there."

"Nah, you said I couldn't get all this gushy wetness on my dick, right?"

"Baby, please just keeping hit that spot."

"Oh, you mean this one," he said, thrusting harder.

"Yesses, Bishop, yes, I'm about to cum."

"Word, say less." He pulled out of me and lifted my ass up to his face, and attacked my pussy with his mouth. His tongue taking the place of his dick Bishop sucked the soul out of me.

"Bishhhhhoppppp," I tried to whisper, but this man was killing my body.

"Fuck my face Kei'."

Lord, when you were making this nigga did you add an extra shot of nasty?

Slapping my ass, Bishop said, "Kei didn't I say fuck my face?

Throw that ass back on my face now."

He didn't have to tell me twice. I started twerking my ass as best

I could since Bishop had me damn near in the air.

"I'm cumming," I said just above a whisper.

"Word. Say less." And just like last time, Bishop stopped, but

this time, he slammed his dick back inside of me.

"Oh my God, Bishop, what are you doing to me?"

"Giving your freak ass what you really want. Now, do you want

a boy or a girl?" He asked before pulling his dick all the way out

until only the tip was at my opening, then thrusting that big ass

thing back inside of me.

"Ugh!!! Twins, I screamed!"

We got banned from Target that day.

'Well, it's about time I get to see y'all freak asses," I said, sitting

down in the booth with my girls.

"Bitch, didn't you get banned from Target." Eboni was the first

one to say something smart.

"And Harris Teeter." Followed by Lo's smart ass.

"And let's not forget Applebee's while mommy and daddy were with them," Renz said, laughing.

"Ard now don't come for me."

"Shit, you cum enough for all of us. You going be just like that one over there working on your 7th child," Lay added, pointing at Eboni.

"Lay shut up, didn't you have a pregnancy scare last month."

"A scare Eboni, not a pregnancy. I mean, do you and Trev be bored in the house? Get a damn puppy or something."

"Okay, Ms. Two kids by two baby daddies working on the third."

"Oh, you tried it, fertile myrtle."

We all laughed. "I miss you, hoes. What's been up?" I asked.

We were having lunch at Friday's in Mondawmin today. The guys had all the kids, so it was a girl's day. Lo, Renz, Lay, Eboni, Tiff, and I decided to eat and shop. Lo, and Renz fake hood asses liked this mall. I personally hated it but whatever.

"So, Malibu's most wanted, why y'all got us at this ghetto ass mall," Eboni questioned, drinking from her virgin strawberry daiquiri.

"Bitch, no, you didn't call them that." I damn near spit my drink out laughing.

"Eboni, just because you, the Ghetto Princess of Harford Rd, don't make us fake. Anyway, we are here because a little birdie told me that a chick named Nicole worked in the Footlocker in here," Renz said, looking at me.

"Stop lying. Let's go now," Lay suggested, getting up from her seat.

"Calm down, Lay. Renz, how you find that out?" I asked.

"Come on, Kei' have you seen our family? Hell, if Paul can get the answers to the SAT questions for Pride, it was nothing to find out where this trick worked at."

Renz was right, but I wasn't worried about this girl. She still was texting Bishop even after he pointed a gun at her head. Clearly, she needs mental help, ain't no way I'm let a nigga slap me, put me out, and raise a gun at me, and I still be blowing him up.

"Kei' you good?"

"Yeah, now y'all know I far from a scared bitch, but after that whole mess with Eric, I'm not trying to deal with any more mentally unstable people. Let that girl live."

"Kei' you sure?" Eboni questioned.

"Yeah, I got my nigga, we straight. But we can still go shop if y'all want, and Lolo give me that damn lighter."

"I wasn't going to set the girl on fire," Lo said, passing me the lighter. "You better take Renz .22 too."

"Renz!"

"What, Kei'? I was just going shoot her in her pinky toe."

"You don't get to hang with Bishop no damn more," I said, shaking my head. "Let's go."

We left the table after paying our bill and leaving a nice tip. We strolled around the mall for like an hour. It wasn't really anything in there for me. I did get some leggings from Forever 21, though.

"Well, well, well, if it isn't the weak bitch that tried to kill herself because her nigga was leaving her pressed ass."

We all turned around to see Nicole standing next to two other females. All three of them were wearing footlocker uniforms, giggling at the comment Nicole just made.

"Bitch, what you say?" Lolo was the first person to say something.

"She heard what the fuck I said. I mean, I guess I get it; the nigga dick is huge, and he definitely cashes out on a bitch," she stated, giving her homegirl a high five.

"Please, Kei' Let me light this bitch up," Lo leaned in and whispered in my ear.

"Nah, it's all good. I got this. Nicole, right? Now please tell the class how my nigga not only slapped your ass and put you out, he also was about to kill your retarded ass, but I saved you.

Yeah, he let you suck his dick and took you to Florida, but

sweetie, it's up for you, so run along before you really get your

feelings hurt."

"Bitch miss me with that bull shit. He told me he only did all that

shit so you wouldn't try and kill your stupid ass again. Pathetic

hoe."

"Oh, really, he said that, interesting."

"Yeah bitch, your nigga be in my bed, almost every night telling

me how he's over your weak ass."

"Oh, word Nicole, I be saying that," Bishop asked, walking up

behind dumb, dumber, and dumbest.

"I told y'all he's always there."

"Y-Y-Yeah nigga you said that last night when we came over my

house, see," she said, shoving her phone in my face. She wanted

to show me a picture of him lying in her bed.

"Now I know you bat shit crazy. Girl, that picture is over a year

old," I laughed. Bishop was, in fact, in her bed, but that's from

the night he came back from Florida.

"No, it's not Bitch."

"Let me just shoot her in her pinky toe, Kei'," Renz said.

"Nicole, I'm going to talk to you like you may have an ounce of sanity in you. "You see his chest. On your phone, it's blank. Now look at his chest now," I said, lifting his shirt. "It says Llaves del Blanco, which means Keys to the Bank. He got that tattoo a week after I came back dumb hoe. I'm the Key; he's the Bank. Bitch I got his heart, and all you ever got was to play with his kids. Now step off before I let my sisters at that ass."

"Bitch don't talk to my friend like that," the short, fat one said.

"Bitch fuck you and your friend," Lay added.

"Whatever, you still a weak bitch, and I could take his ass any day of the week," Nicole said. Nicole folded her arms as if I was supposed to be bothered by what she just said.

"Oh, really, you think so? Let's test that theory, Bishop."

"Sup, babe."

"Can she, have you?"

"Fuck no. I don't even understand why you are giving this annoying hoe this much conversation."

"Just cause he said no in your face, don't mean shit," Nicole snapped.

"You are so right," I responded.

"Bishop, up."

Without hesitation, Bishop picked me up on his shoulders and slid his tongue up and down my panties in the middle of the mall.

"You still want him, Nicole?"

"Fuck both of y'all," she said, storming off.

"Are y'all niggas crazy?" Renz said, shaking her head.

"Put me down, Bishop."

"Crazy bout mine," he said, licking my juices off his top lip.

"It's something really wrong with the both of y'all. I'm telling momma," Lolo stated as she walked away from us.

"That shit was hot. Let me call my nigga and tell him to meet me now. A bitch is ready to bust it wide open," Eboni's pregnant ass said, looking for her phone.

"Hey Kei' let me holla at you really quick," Bishop requested, pulling my hand in the direction of the elevators.

"The bathrooms dirty as shit down here but upstairs should be empty."

"Don't get banned from here too with y'all nasty asses," Renz warned.

We laughed and took our lil nasty asses upstairs, where I came all in Bishop's mouth. Something about that man I just can't get enough of.

"Mommy, I didn't want to hit grandma, but she was hurting KJ."

"Bri'annna, you not supposed to hit period, especially not grown-ups or your family."

"But mommy, KJ was crying, and I got to protect her."

"Bri'annna, your sister's teeth are growing, so she's going to be cranky, and Grandma has nothing to do with that. But you can't go around hitting people."

"But mommy BJ said I'm the big sister."

"Baby, I understand that, but you can't hit your grandmother. Now go get that iPad and put it in our room."

"But mommy..."

"No buts Bri'annna Gabriella Blanca now go!"

Bri'annna stormed off in the direction of her room. That little girl will have me catching charges and bailing out her father.

"Why is my daughter crying in our bed?" Bishop asked as he carried KJ in his arms.

"Because she hit your mother-in-law."

"Well, what mom dukes do?"

"Bishop!" I screamed. "She didn't do anything, and even if she did, Bri' is a child."

"Bri' come here"

"Yes, daddy."

"Why did you hit your grandmother?"

"Because KJ was crying when she was holding her. Daddy, I thought she was hurting her," she answered, putting her head down.

"Bri' lift your head up and look at daddy. Now KJ is teething, so she's going be cranky, and that's nobody's fault, okay."

"Yes, daddy."

"And what did daddy tell you about hitting people?"

"You said shoot them in the pinky toe?"

"Bishop!"

"What? Was I wrong?"

"You know damn well; she can't go around shooting people."

"Why the fuck not, soon as she can see over the counter, I'm taking her straight to the gun range."

"You are fucking crazy."

"Crazy for mine."

"Daddy, mommy said I couldn't have my iPad."

"Bri'annna, I'm not scared of your daddy."

"Bri' Bri' go watch a movie in your room really quick."

"Kei' let me holla at your right quick," he asked, licking his lips.

Needless to say, Bri'annna got her iPad back.

Bankz

"Yo Kei', how much you know about Lay's baby father?"

"Who Si'?"

"Yeah him."

"Nothing. Why?"

"The nigga came at me last night looking for Sin, talking bout he not taking his spot as HC daddy. Nigga was talking reckless, and before I holla at Sin, I want to see if he's worth getting at."

"Babe, Si' has been a clown since the day I met him. You know he used to beat on Lay and HC too."

"Fuck, you just say? He did what?" I picked up my phone and called Sin.

"Bro, is Lay near you?"

"Nigga why are you looking for my woman?"

"Boy, don't nobody want Lay high yellow ass. Is she near you?"

"Yeah, man, damn."

"Put me on speaker."

"Bishop, you don't have to do all this." Kei' was trying to defuse the shit before it started.

"Kei' go sit down somewhere."

"What's up Bankz?" Lay said, sounding like she was away from the phone.

"Lil sis, that nigga Si' use to beat on you and lil man?

"Lay, I swear I thought Sin knew already," Kei' hollered into the phone.

"I know you are not talking about that nut ass nigga that Lay just had my son around," Sin hollered.

"Sin, it's not that deep, it was years ago, and he is HC daddy."

"Lay, as much as I love you, if you ever refer to anyone else as my son's father, I'll kill you and raise the kids as a single father."

"What the fuck is wrong with this family?" Kei' asked, shaking my head.

"Lay, did he or didn't he beat on you and Harlem?" I was getting annoyed.

"Bankz, he umm I mean he..." Lay was stumbling over her words.

"Bro, what you wanna do?" I questioned, cutting Lay off.

"Well, after I cuss my future wife out for holding this information, I'll meet you at the gym."

"Bet, hey yo, we still taking the girls to Disney on Ice?"

"Are you for real Bishop, y'all talking about possibly killing someone than in the same breath you asking about Disney on Ice?" Kei' inquired like I was wrong or something.

"Yeah, what's wrong with that?"

"I can't with you."

"Bro, I'll see you at the gym," Sin said, hanging up.

Lay fucked with some nutball ass niggas; I thought as I walked out of the house.

"Sin, how are we handling this Si' nigga?" I asked soon as I entered the gym.

"Dead that nigga, HC doesn't need him. He got me."

"Say less when are you trying to handle this shit?"

"After the wedding."

"Who's wedding nigga?"

"Mine. I'm ready to make Lay my wife and adopt Harlem and Brooklyn."

"That's what the fuck I'm talking about," I said, giving him dap.

"Yo, on some real shit, I been looking at the houses down by the harbor, and I'm about to buy Lay one. It's like six more for sale, and I thought maybe we should all just move down there," Sin suggested, adding more weights to the bar.

"You for real? What the numbers look like?"

"Decent, bro. I talked to Trev and Moshi about it, and they're down."

"Well, shit, we should just buy the whole compound," I stated, ready to move today!

"I got Tiff coming over to set the buy up in an hour. She doesn't know all the details; she just thinks we all going into business with each other." Sin was always on point when it came to investments and shit like that. I trusted him with my life, so if he said the numbers were good, I was down.

"Bet, she got everyone's account information anyway. We should throw in a new car in there for the ladies."

"Just one car Bankz. Don't be trying to buy the car lot out."

"Nigga shut up and lift the damn weights; I got this"

Kei'sha

"Lay, calm down, please I can't understand you while you are crying and screaming."

"Kei' I fucked up, I didn't tell Sin the truth about Si,' and now he's leaving me."

"Lay Sin is not going anywhere," I reassured her.

"Yes, he is. I didn't tell you that I let Harlem go with Si' for a day, and Si' took all the money off Harlem's bank card Sin gave him. I tried to sneak and put the money back on the card, but you know Harlem tells Sin everything. Now he's leaving me for good, Kei' he packed up the whole house, he's not answering the phone, and he took the kids out of school early. I can't believe this shit."

"I'm on my way to you. Just calm down, please."

I told Sin and Bishop this was a bad idea, but nooooo, no one listens to Kei'sha. This fool Sin wanted to surprise Lay with a new house, and his idea was to pretend he was leaving her and taking the kids. We all know Lay has not had it easy with men.

Over the years, she developed anxiety and insecurities. Sin was like a knight in shining armor for her. Why he wanted to play like this was beyond me.

"Kei' can he take my kids?" Lay asked, still crying and getting on my damn nerves at this point.

"He's not taking your damn kids, Lay, and legally no, he can't. He has no rights to them."

"I just can't believe my life right now. I didn't tell Sin what Si did to me because I knew he would kill him, and I didn't want Sin to get in any trouble. I don't want to lose Sin. He's the best thing that ever happened to us. You know HC calls him Dad, and he's all Brooklynn knows as a father."

"Lay, it'll be okay. Try calling him again."

She picked up her iPhone and called him. This time he answered.

"Sin, baby, where are you? What's all that music?"

"What? Put it on speaker," I demanded.

We heard loud music and Sin talking to some girl. What made my neck snap was my damn husband's voice in the background asking some bitch if she was going to swallow his babies.

"Oh, fuck no," I said, picking up my phone to call my husband. The bastard didn't answer. I went to my Find My Phone app to see where his ass was.

Lay sat on the passenger side, crying even harder.

"Lay shut the fuck up, damn it. I need you to grow some balls because if these niggas on some weird shit, I'm killing them both," I said. I reached over her to get the gun Bishop made me keep in my car for emergencies from out of the glove department.

Lay got her shit together and took the safety off her .22. "You right, Kei, it's up for these niggas I swear."

We got to their location within 15 minutes.

"Oh, they fucking with rich bitches I see," I said, pulling up to a gated community close to Fells Point.

"Look, Kei' there goes Sin truck, pull over!"

Before I had the car in park, Lay jumped out of the car and was

taking the steps two at a time. Getting to the top of the house's

stairs, Sin's truck was parked in front. Lay was about to knock on

the door, but I stopped her.

"Nah, we not giving them a chance to even try to lie." With that

said, I aimed my gun and shot that fucking door down. Bishop

had me fucked up!

"Sin, I swear I'm going to kill your ass," Lay said as we kicked the

rest of the door down.

When we got in, the first room was empty, so we walked

towards the back of the house. What we saw had us stopping in

our tracks. The room was filled with our family and friends,

yellow and cream roses, candles all around the room. Sin was

down on one knee, standing beside him was HC and Brooklynn

with signs that said, "He stole our momma's heart, so we are

stealing his last name."

"Oh my god!" Lay cried.

"Lay, I never thought I'd be the type nigga to get married and have kids, but you changed me. You make a nigga want to come home and watch Lifetime." We all laughed. Lay always had us watching Lifetime movies. "On some real shit, I want this forever, my Goodie. Will you fuck with your nigga the long way?"

"Yes, yes, yes!"

We all screamed and ran to Lay to inspect the ring.

"Ummm, gangster Kei' are you paying for my damn door too?"

"Kei' why would you shoot the door, ma?" Bishop asked.

"Nigga I thought y'all was in here with some bitches." I shrugged my shoulders.

"Sin, what do you mean pay for your door?" Lay asked, still admiring her ring.

"I was getting to that, Bishop, Trevor, Moshi, y'all ready?"

"Let's do it," they said.

"Do what?" I asked.

Bishop came over to me while all the other guys stood next to their girls.

"When I first met all y'all, I wasn't feeling it. I have always been a one-man show; besides Sin, I never fucked with a bunch of niggas. I didn't know Kei' had such a big family. But thanks to Kei' I found my family, and a nigga is blessed to have y'all in his life on some G shit; I love y'all niggas. Y'all became the brothers I never wanted," he laughed. "And the little sisters I'll go to war for. With that said, me and my brothers decided it's no point of us all living in different areas when our kids have play dates every fucking day, and our ladies can't go a day without seeing each other."

"Ladies welcome home," Trevor and Moshi said together.

When he said that, each guy gave us a key with a keychain picture on it. It was a picture of all the kids in cute matching outfits.

"Now go outside, and each house has a car in front of it. Find your car, and you'll find your house." Sin gave directions.

We ran out of the house in search of our new home.

"I found mine!" Eboni said, standing next to a white 2019 Mercedes- Benz Sprinter van on her license plate said, T.E.A.M 7.

"Trevor, why the fuck you buy my sister a sprinter van?" Purnell yelled out of the house.

"Nigga we got seven kids. What else could I get her beside a magic school bus?"

We laughed so hard. It was true she couldn't get a regular car.

"I found my car," Lay said. Sin brought her a 2019 BMW X7. The license plate said, "Goodie."

"Sinnnnn, oh my god!" On the hood of her car was a folder with adoption papers.

"Got mine," Tiff said. She walked towards her 2019 all-white Audi R8 with "Tiff Piff" on her license plate. Moshi cashed out on that damn car.

"Kei' did you find yours?" Eboni asked.

"No, Bishop, where my damn car and house at nigga?"

"Damn Kei' you look like you're upset." His ass was laughing like shit was funny.

"Nah, for real, Kei' let me holla at you for a minute."

"Oh god, that means we bout to get banned from our new community, don't be fucking on the lawn or some weird shit like that," Lay said. She was all hugged up and in Sin's face.

"Shut up and worry about this dick you bout to be bouncing on," Sin added, smacking her butt.

Mmmmm, yes, daddy," she said, giving Sin a wet sloppy kiss."

"No wonder this group stays having babies," our cousin Jen stated, walking out of Sin and Lay's house. "I'm broke, don't invite me to any more baby showers," she said, getting in her car.

I guess our family sick of us and babies, but the way shit goes in the family, I bet my last dollar another round of babies were on the way.

'Bishop, where is my damn house and car?"

"Come on, Kei'," he said, grabbing my hand.

"I swear you are not getting even a whiff of this box if we are not walking to a damn house and car."

"Well damn Kei' what if your nigga couldn't afford all that."

"Nigga shut up, I'm in charge of your books; you can afford all these damn houses," Tiff said, walking behind us with the rest of the group following to.

"Tiff, I'm firing your ass," Bishop said, looking back at her.

"And I'm taking all your money, win-win for me."

"I'm reporting your ass to the ethic community or something," Bishop said, stopping in front of this gorgeous house with a white 2019 Jeep Cherokee High Altitude 4x4, with "Kei2Bank" on the license plate and a 2019 Mercedes- Benz S-class coupe with "BJ4ever" on the licenses plate.

"Nigga we said one damn car and house. Why you gotta be the hardheaded one?" Sin yelled.

"Man, that Jeep was cheap as hell; Kei' been talking about that raggedy-ass truck since I met her, so I had to get it, but I had to get my baby something else."

"I can't believe we all get to live so close to each other. This is so dope, and the all-white theme y'all got going on is hot," Tiff said.

"Now make sure y'all share y'all toys and play nice with each other," Moshi demanded, sounding like somebody's damn daddy.

"Oh, hush it," Tiff said, giving him a kiss.

"Yo Kei' let me holla at you real quick. I wanna show you the balcony," Bishop stated while holding my hand and walking towards our new home.

"Y'all better not be fucking on that front balcony. I don't wanna step out to get my morning paper and see you sticking dick in lil sis," Sin joked.

"Nigga you don't even read the paper, so shut up."

We walked into our house and fucked in each room, including bathrooms, closets, pantries, and all three balconies' the house had. Yeah, another round of babies was coming soon.

"Bri' Bri', are you ready to see all your guests?"

"Mommy, can KJ wear the same thing as me?"

"Bri' Bri', we talked about this; it's your day. KJ will have the same colors on, but that's it."

"Okay, mommy, can I get her dressed?"

"Sure, Bri' Bri'."

"Oh, and mommy, can you stop calling me Bri' Bri'? I'm six now and a big girl."

I laughed, "Of course, baby, what would you like mommy to call you?"

"Just Bri' mommy."

"Okay, baby, I can do that."

"Thanks, mommy." She ran out of the room towards her sister's room.

Today was her big 6th birthday party, and she was so excited. This party has gone beyond my wildest dreams. Once Bishop started talking about live animals, I cut ties with him and the party planners.

"I'm going to shoot this nigga right in his pinky toe," Bishop said, walking into our room.

"What's wrong, babe?"

"Your brother, he going buy Bri' the same BMW ride-on toy I brought her and won't take his back."

"So, you want to kill my brother over a toy?"

"I didn't say kill. I said I was going to shoot him in his pinky toe."

"Bishop, you are crazy."

"Crazy bout mine always. That's what you're wearing to the party?"

"Yeah, why?"

"Ummm, you don't see your ass hanging out of them shorts?"

"Bishop, it's a pool party."

"Only way you get to wear those out this house is if you come holla at me real quick," he stated, licking them sexy ass lips.

"No, hell no! The party starts in one hour."

"Well, you better get over here quick than," he suggested, tilting his head to the side.

"Nah, I'll change," I said, going back in the closet to find something else to put on. When I turned around to take the shorts off, Bishop slammed his dick inside of me. I didn't even hear him walking up to me

"Bishop, you can't keep doing this to meee. Oh god, why do you feel so good?"

"Because this dick was made for you, now fuck me, Kei'."

Bishop used his long arm to pull the chair in the corner of our closet under him and sat down without letting his dick slip out of me.

"Fuck me, Kei'" he said. He slapped my ass; while sitting on him reverse cowgirl style, I bent down and grabbed my ankles and started bouncing up and down on him.

"Yeah, just like that, that ass getting big, bounced that shit Kei'."
He slapped my ass

"Bishop, I swear you going on a pussy diet; this don't make no sense." I was talking shit. I wasn't depriving this man of a damn thing.

"Oh word, say less."

Now, why would I fucking say that shit? This man lifted me up off the chair, threw my ass across the island we had in here, and ate my ass like he was on death row, and I was his last meal.

"Kei' you know damn well I'm getting this pussy whenever I want," he said, all the while his face was still buried in my ass.

"Bishop, I'm sorry. Oh shit, I'm about to cum."

"Cum in my mouth Kei." I did just that. I was knocking over all the clothes that were folded as I did.

"Now come suck, daddy dick."

I loved sucking Bishop's dick. That got me super wet. Bishop's dick was a perfect fit in my mouth. I loved how it touched the back of my throat and when he would pull his dick out and smack my face with it, I creamed so bad.

"And you better make it sloppy," he demanded, pulling my hair.

"Si'papi."

Spitting on his dick, I didn't play any games. Deep-throating that big ass thing was one of my greatest accomplishments. Using my hand, I started playing with his balls while going crazy on his dick.

"You nasty lil bitch, suck daddy dick," he stated, slapping my face.

"Ughhh, Bishop cum in my mouth."

"Say less."

He started fucking my face while I took my other hand and started rubbing on my clit.

"Nah, move your hand. I got something better."

While I was still sucking his dick, Bishop went into the draw on the island; that's where I keep all our sex toys. Pulling out the silver bullet Bishop put it on the max speed.

"Turn over on your back," he demanded, as I was lying on the island with his dick in my mouth.

"If my dick comes out your mouth, I'm not fucking you for two weeks."

My eyes bulged. I never want to go that long without Bishop's dick in me, near me, hell at night, sometimes I wake up and just smell it. I am obsessed with that thing. I turned over, holding Bishop in my mouth as my life depended on it.

"Now open them legs wide, and if you stop sucking, you know what the consequences will be, right?" He reached over me and put the bullet right on my clit.

I shook my head, acknowledging I understood. As soon as that bullet hit my clit I was done.

"Now I know I said you better keep sucking; maybe this little sliver friend of yours is a distraction," he said, turning it off.

"No, Bishop, I promise I'll keep sucking; just turn it back on, please." I was begging at this point. The things this man did to my body had to be illegal.

"Kei' you got two minutes to make me bust a big as nut on that pretty face, or you're punished," he said, turning the bullet back on.

I sucked his dick so nasty and sloppy; Bishop was damn near scramming like a bitch. Thanks to the bullet still being on my clit I had cum like three times.

"Kei' I'm about to cum. Where you want it?"

"Semen en mi pepquena boca desagradable papi."

"Say less." He pulled my hair, forcing my head to go back a little more, then unloaded his kids down my throat.

"Damn Kei' that shit was the truth."

Knock Knock, "Mommy, Daddy, we ready. It's time for my party."

Oh, shit, we jumped up; I'm glad we locked our bedroom door.

"Damn, we forgot about the fucking party," Bishop said, heading towards the bathroom.

I was right behind him, shaking my head. We needed to get our shit together.

"Mommy, mommy, uncle Dam got me a present. Can I open it now?" Bri' came running with Dam walking behind her, holding KJ.

"Bri' you got a table full of gifts. This one can wait like the rest of them."

"Please, mommy. Uncle Dam asked me what I wanted and said I could have anything, so I wanna see if he got it."

"Come on, lil sis, let her open it," Dam requested with this dumb-ass grin on his face.

"Okay, Bri' you can open it."

"Yeahhh," she screamed as she tore the paper off the box.

"Yes, thank you, Uncle Dam!"

"Damall Wilson! I know damn well you didn't buy my daughter a gun! Bishop, get over here!"

Bishop, Sin, Moshi, and Trevor walked over to where we were standing.

"What's wrong, Kei'?"

"Look what this fool got our 6-year-old," I said, pointing to the baby .38 wrapped in a hello kitty shell.

"Nigga, that's the one I got her," Sin said.

"You mean to tell me you bought her one too?"

"Shit she asked."

"Who else in this damn group brought my child a gun?"

They all raised their hand except Trevor.

"Kei' I didn't get her a gun," he said.

"I'm glad someone has some sense."

"She just asked me for bullets," he stated.

"Y'all got 2.5 seconds to get out my damn face. I can't believe y'all. She's six. What could she possibly do with four guns, start a toddler mafia?" I was vexed!

"Pinky toe, pinky toe," KJ said in her small three-year-old voice.

"Oh no, not you too. Bishop, you got my daughters thinking it's cool to shoot people in their pinky toe."

"What? It's not?"

"Ugh, I'm divorcing you and them damn ready for war kids," I said, walking off. I heard them laughing.

"Do y'all know these fools brought Bri' Hello Kitty guns?" I was sitting by the pool talking to my girls.

"Them niggas straight copied me," Renz said.

"Renz, not you too. What the fuck is wrong with this family?"

"I didn't buy her a gun," Lolo added.

"Let me guess you brought bullets?"

"Nope, a blow torch."

It's something really wrong with all of y'all.

"GET AWAY FROM MY SISTER!"

We heard Bri' scream, but before we got to her, we heard a gunshot.

"Bishopppppp," I screamed.

We all ran over to where Bri' and KJ were standing.

"Daddy, I did it. I shot her in her pinky toe. You said we don't hit, so I did what you said."

KJ stood next to her, clapping her damn hands.

"Bri'annna, oh my god, come here," I said, walking closer towards her and KJ.

"Mommy, I did it, she was grabbing KJ, and I don't know her."

"Bri' how did you know how to shoot the gun?"

"Daddy taught me; he takes me to BJ's every time you have ladies' day with aunties."

"Bishop, I swear I'm divorcing your ass. Why are you taking Bri'annna? You know what, never mind Bri' take your sister in the house with GG and Pop Pop."

"Okay, mommy, KJ, you wanna hold my gun?"

"Oh, hell no, Bri' give me that damn gun."

"Anybody want to explain to me how my 6-year-old got hold of a loaded gun, and who the bitch is she just shot?"

"Ain't that the bitch Nicole?" I heard Renz say.

"Bitch have you lost your mind, coming to my house, putting your hands on my daughter."

"Fuck them bastard ass kids, Bishop. I was there when this weak bitch tried to kill herself and left your ass, but you choose her over me? I loved you."

Pow!

We all looked up and saw my mother standing in the window next to the backyard holding a Smith and Wesson.

"Bishop, I told you to get rid of her a year ago. You just don't listen."

"I'm sorry, Mom Dukes; I thought for sure she wasn't going be a problem."

"Well, she ain't now," Dam said. "Come on, let us go get some cake."

"Cake! Are you fucking serious? You know what, I want out of this damn family. Y'all are bat shit crazy. Bishop, our daughter, just shot someone!"

"I know, that shit was gangster as hell. Her aim was on point too," he said, smiling like a proud father. As if his daughter just got accepted into Yale or something.

"Hey, hello, people, am I the only one that realizes how horrible this whole situation is? Not only did Bri' shoot someone, there is a dead body in my fucking backyard."

"Kei' baby, calm down, we own this whole compound nobody saw anything except us, the cleanup crew is on their way, and it's only family at this party. We straight," Bishop replied,

hugging me.

"Lil sis, you got to admit, Bri' did that."

"Trevor, shut your ass up," Eboni said, elbowing him in his side.

"Y'all get in here so we can sing Happy Birthday," my mom

demanded, hollering out the window. Everyone started walking

towards the back door.

"Hey Kei' let me holla at you right quick."

"Oh, shit, there they go, y'all just nasty!" Lolo said, shaking her

head.

"Bishop, we can wait to the party over, babe."

"Ard bet, just know for every hour I gotta wait that's how many

times I'm making you cum," he whispered in my ear.

Lord, this man was going be the death of me.

"So Bri' did you enjoy your birthday?"

We were all lying in our King size bed watching Frozen for the

millionth time.

"Yes, mommy, I did. Do I get to keep all my guns?"

"We are going to put them in a safe place until you are a little older," Bishop responded.

"Aww, man, Daddy, can I just keep one?"

"You can take one with us when we go to the gun range, and only in there can you use it."

"But daddy."

"No, but's Bri'."

"Okay, daddy."

"Mommy, when are you going to give me my other present?"

"What present, Bri'?"

"The one BJ said was coming."

Looking at my daughter, I was surprised and scared at the same time, oddly.

"Do you want me to tell daddy?"

"Tell Daddy what?"

"My brothers are coming."

Bishop looked at me with the biggest grin I've ever seen.

"Bri'annna, it's time for bed," I said, trying to get out of the conversation.

"Aww, Mommy, can we sleep in here, please?"

"Only because it's your birthday."

"Kei' we need to talk about this gift," Bishop suggested as he laid a sleeping KJ on the bed.

"We will once Bri' go to sleep."

I didn't realize we all fell asleep watching the movie. I woke up around 2 am to go to the bathroom. After using it and washing my hands, I went to the side of the bed Bishop was lying on and bent down to smell his dick like I did every night.

"You know that's creepy as hell, right?" Bishop said, scaring the shit out of me.

"I didn't know you were woke."

"Kei' I feel you sniffing me every night. Why do you do that?"

"I don't know; I just do," I replied, laughing, walking towards my side of the bed.

"Nah." Bishop grabbed my arm.

"Let me holla at you right quick," he said, licking his lips.

"Where are you taking me?" I asked as we walked down the steps and out the door.

"I have been wanting to do this since they brought this bitch here this morning," Bishop laughed, walking into the bouncy house.

"I can't believe you want to have sex in this damn bouncy house."

"Have sex. Who said that? I just wanted to jump in this bitch. I have never been inside one, but since you brought up sex, come jump on this dick," he demanded, sitting down in the middle of the bouncy house.

"You are crazy," I said, shaking my head.

"Crazy bout mine now get over here. Didn't I say for every hour you made me wait, I'm going to make you cum? The party ended at 7 pm its 3 am now that's 8 hours, so you ready to come eight times?"

"You wish you could make me cum eight times."

"Oh, is that a challenge, Mrs. Blanca?"

"Oh yes, it is Mr. Blanca."

"Now, before I fuck your little brains out, tell me about my sons."

"Well, I'm only 11 weeks, but I had them do an early genetic test, and Bri' was right; she will have two little brothers."

"Kei' thank you so much, baby. I swear I love you and will always be here for you and our kids."

"I'm glad you said that because it's not just two babies coming."

"Kei' stop playing we having triplets? Damn, I got that Trevor nut."

"Bishop, we are having quadruplets, two boys and two girls."

"Get the fuck out of here, damn baby, you stuck with my ass now."

"Bishop, we have to get Bri' some therapy."

"Fuck, my daughter needs therapy for?"

"Bishop, you don't think it's strange that she carries full-blown conversations with her dead brother, likes guns, shoots people, and has an unorthodox relationship with her sister? I can only imagine how she is going to act with these new ones coming. Not to mention she doesn't play about her cousins either."

"Kei' she shot one person, so far."

"That's all you heard?"

"I agree her talking to BJ is kind of scary, but that other shit doesn't phase me."

"Really, Bishop?"

"Shhh, that's not why we came out here. We can discuss that later. Get over here so I can make you cum eight times and put four more babies up in you," he said, pulling out our silver bullet from his pajama pants pocket.

"You are crazy," I laughed.

"Crazy bout mine always."

The End

What's up world. I know, I know we put y'all through a lot, right.

Blame my girl Erica for that. I hope you enjoyed our story; we

won't be gone for too long. It's some more dysfunctional

members of this family y'all gotta read about, then the big

wedding for Sin and Lay.

"Hey Kei' let me holla at you real quick."

Well, guys, y'all know what that means. I gotta go! See ya later.

CPSIA information can be obtained
at www.ICGtesting.com
Printed in the USA
LVHW041545150621
690286LV00003B/369